KB085290

아들

아시아에서는 《바이링궐 에디션 한국 대표 소설》을 기획하여 한국의 우수한 문학을 주제별로 엄선해 국내외 독자들에게 소개합니다. 이 기획은 국내외 우수한 번역가들이 참여하여 원작의 품격을 최대한 살렸습니다. 문학을 통해 아시아의 정체성과 가치를 살피는 데 주력해 온 아시아는 한국인의 삶을 넓고 깊게 이해하는 데 이 기획이 기여하기를 기대합니다.

Asia Publishers presents some of the very best modern Korean literature to readers worldwide through its new Korean literature series ⟨Bilingual Edition Modern Korean Literature⟩. We are proud and happy to offer it in the most authoritative translation by renowned translators of Korean literature. We hope that this series helps to build solid bridges between citizens of the world and Koreans through a rich in-depth understanding of Korea.

바이링궐 에디션 한국 대표 소설 077

Bi-lingual Edition Modern Korean Literature 077

Father and Son

윤정모

아들

Yoon Jung-mo

ASIA
PUBLISHERS

Contents

아들   007
Father and Son

해설   079
Afterword

비평의 목소리   089
Critical Acclaim

작가 소개   098
About the Author

아들

Father and Son

분수대를 한 바퀴 돌았다. 아들놈은 보이지 않았다. 그는 사방을 두리번거렸다. 노인들이 한가롭게 앉아 있는 계단 그 위쪽에서 젊은 여인이 아기의 손을 잡고 내려오고 있었다. 아기는 갓 돌이 지난 듯했고, 젊은 엄마는 꼬마의 서툰 걸음마를 도와 천천히 계단을 밟아 내렸다. 그의 입가에 미소가 떠올랐다. 그는 그쪽을 향해 한 발 내딛었다.

그때 건물 꼭대기에서 해가 불쑥 고개를 내밀며 그의 시야를 가로막았다. 그는 눈을 가리고 주춤 뒤로 물러났다. 잠시 눈앞이 캄캄했다. 그는 다시 볼 수 있을 때까

The man made a loop around the fountain, but didn't see his son anywhere. He looked in every direction. Some seniors were sitting around on the stairs, and a young woman was coming down from above, holding her baby's hand. The child appeared to be just over a year old, and the young mom was walking slowly, helping him with each tottering step. The ends of the man's lips rose, and he took a step toward them.

Then suddenly the sun came poking its head over the building, its light obstructing his view. He shielded his eyes and shrank back. Everything went black for a moment. He blinked a few times until

지 몇 번이나 눈을 껌벅거렸다. 이 무슨 착각인가. 그는 세차게 머리를 흔들며 이번엔 계단 쪽이 아니라 북쪽 건물을 쳐다보았다. 거기 건물 시계가 있었다. 빨간 전 광판으로 된 숫자가 아홉 시 사십구 분에서 막 오십 분 으로 바뀌고 있었다.

십 분 전이군. 그는 가방을 추스르고 분수대 난간에 걸터앉았다. 아내는 매사에 애발라서 육아에도 극성이 었다. 어디서 주워들었는지 태교 운운하면서 임신 중 한참이나 부부관계를 거부하더니 백일 수수떡을 해먹 고부터는 자주 나들이를 강요했었다. 무엇이든 많이 본 애가 똑똑하다구요. 그 말은 아내의 전주곡이었다. 딴 은 창경원 하마를 보고 어린 놈이 좋아할 땐 아내가 아 기의 마음을 척척 알아내는 요술쟁이 같기도 했었다. 그는 가방을 무릎에 올렸다. 그 속엔 김밥과 찐 계란, 도 넛과 우유 등이 들어 있다. 아들놈과 대공원에서 먹을 것들이었다. 그는 이 음식들을 사는 데도 꼬박 사오십 분을 잡아먹었다. 하긴 서울 지리도 많이 달라졌어. 전 에 없던 건물들이 길을 턱턱 막아섰으니……. 한데 이 녀석은?

he could see again. Was he hallucinating? He whirled back around, this time to look at the building to the north, not the stairs. That's where the clock was. The red electronic digits were just changing from 9:49 to 9:50.

Ten minutes to go. He adjusted his bag and perched himself on the fountain guardrail. His wife was cautious about everything; with childcare, too, she'd gone to great extremes. He didn't know where she'd picked up her ideas: for the sake of the baby, she forbade sex for a while when she was pregnant, and from the moment they first ate rice cakes to celebrate his 100th day in the world, she often demanded they go on outings. "A baby who sees a lot is smart, you know, no matter what it is he sees." This was their cue to embark on another outing.

Actually she seemed like a magician, able to read the baby's mind. She just *knew* he'd enjoy seeing the hippo at Changgyeong Park.[1] The man rested the bag on his lap. Inside was *kimbap*, hard-boiled eggs, doughnuts and milk—snacks for the child and him to share at the park. He'd taken a good forty or fifty minutes buying them. Seoul had really changed a lot. Buildings that hadn't even existed before now

그는 벌떡 일어나 주변을 살펴보았다. 아무도 없었다. 다시 시계를 올려다보았다. 오십오 분이었다. 그런데 이 앤 버스를 타고 올까 아니면 지하철? 그 방향도 지하철이 개통되었나? 어쨌거나 좀 늦을 수도 있겠지. 아직 오 분 전이었지만 그는 그런 생각을 했다. 자기 역시도 새벽부터 서둘렀지만 종각에 내렸을 땐 아홉 시였음을 상기했다.

그는 난간에 도로 앉아 가방의 지퍼를 열고 내용물을 살펴보았다. 도넛과 우유도 흐트러짐 없이 그대로 들어 있었다. 그는 안심하고 다시 지퍼를 채웠다. 그리고 그는 또 한 번 주위를 돌아본 후 손을 머리로 가져갔다. 모자는 똑바로 씌워져 있었다. 문득 아들의 고수머리가 떠올랐다.

십일 년 전이던가. 아들을 순산했다는 전갈을 받고 집으로 달려갔을 때 아내는 혼곤히 잠들어 있었고, 그 옆엔 배내옷에 싸인 갓난애가 고물고물 움직이고 있었다. 그렇게 신기한 일이 세상에 또 있을까. 아기의 머리카락이 흡사 파마를 한 듯 동글동글 말려 있는 게 아닌가. 그는 그만 웃음을 터뜨리고 말았다. 그 바람에 잠이 깬

choked the streets... But where was that kid, anyway?

The man sprang to his feet and looked carefully around, but couldn't see anybody. He glanced up at the clock again. It was 9:55. Would the boy come by bus or by subway? Was there a subway line coming from his direction? The boy *could* be a little late. He was entertaining the possibility even at five minutes to the hour. He reminded himself that in his own case, he'd risen at dawn to get ready but hadn't arrived in Jonggak until nine.

He sank back down on the rail, unzipped the bag, and checked inside. The doughnuts and milk were there and intact. Relieved, he did it up again. After looking around once more, he lifted his hand to his head. His hat was on straight. Suddenly he thought of his son's curly hair.

About eleven years ago, he'd received the call—his wife had safely given birth to a baby boy. He came racing home to find his wife sleeping, and his newborn son wriggling around in swaddling clothes beside her. He'd never seen anything so amazing. His son had loose coils of hair, just as if his hair had been permed. The man broke out laughing. At that, his wife awoke and gave him a

13

아내가 눈을 흘겼다.

"이이 좀 봐. 애 낳은 사람 고생은 염두에도 없고 자기 머리 닮은 것만 좋아하시네."

그는 또 모자를 만졌다. 그 순간 정문 앞에서 만난 교대근무자의 말이 생각났다.

"오늘 특박인가? 한데 그 모자가 옷에 비해 너무 새거로군."

이 모자는 한 달 전에 출감자에게 부탁해서 차입 받은 것이었다. 그는 그 모자에다 미리 구김살을 만들지 못한 것이 큰 실수처럼 여겨졌다. 마음 같아서는 지금이라도 손질을 하고 싶었지만, 그러나 벗을 수가 없었다. 그는 가방을 둘러메고 돌아서서 분수대를 바라보았다. 하얀 물줄기가 거침없이 뻗어 내렸다. 꽉 막힌 음식물이 내려가듯 조금이나마 가슴속이 후련했다. 그는 오늘 아침에도 잠깐 이런 기분을 맛보았다. 수염을 깎고, 세수를 하고, 아침 관식을 먹고 영치되어 있던 돈과 옷을 찾아 입고 정문을 나서기까지……. 그 과정은 마치 안으로 맴돌기만 하던 물줄기가 비로소 수로를 찾은 것과 같았다.

dirty look.

"Look at you. You don't give a damn what I went through to have this baby, you just like it that his hair resembles yours."

He felt for his hat again. Then he remembered what the guard he'd met in front of the main gate had said.

"You're going on special leave today? Your hat looks out of place. It's too new compared to your clothes."

A month earlier, he'd had a former inmate send him the hat as a favor. He chided himself for not having made creases in it ahead of time. Still self-conscious, he'd have fixed it on the spot, but he couldn't bring himself to take it off. He lifted his bag onto his shoulder and turned to look at the fountain. An arc of white water kept shooting out. He felt a little better inside, as if there was food stuck in his throat and it was now finally going down. Earlier that morning, he'd enjoyed the same feeling for a moment. He'd shaved, washed, eaten his rations, collected his money and street clothes from custody, donned his clothes, and come all the way out the front gate. Yes, with this series of ac-

그러나 겨울이 오면 이 분수 역시도 다시금 갇히고 말겠지…….

그의 얼굴에 성큼 그늘이 다가섰다. 그는 얼른 물에 손을 적셨다. 그리고 그 물을 찍어다 바지의 주름살을 펴기 시작했다.

"아빠."

한 소년이 그를 불렀다. 고수머리였다.

"익수야, 익수구나!"

그는 와락 소년을 껴안았다. 소년에겐 아직도 어릴 때의 냄새가 남아 있었다.

"많이 자랐구나. 많이도…….."

그의 손은 게걸스런 짐승처럼 소년의 팔과 다리를 만져댔다. 익수야, 아빠는 말이다. 너의 살을 만져보는 게 소원이었단다. 그의 손길은 어느새 소년의 엉덩이로 해서 고추 쪽을 더듬고 있었다. 소년은 슬며시 궁둥이를 빼냈다.

"아빠, 남들이 보잖아."

"이 녀석아, 아빠가 아들 고추 만지는 건 흉이 아니야."

tions, it seemed like the water that had been swirling in circles had finally found a channel out.

But when the winter came, the fountain would surely find itself stopped up again.

A shadow flickered over his face. He suddenly wet his hand in the fountain water and began smoothing out wrinkles in his pants.

A boy called out, "Dad." A curly-haired boy.

"Ik-su. It's you!"

He threw his arms around the child. Ik-su still had the scent he'd had as a baby.

"You've grown so much. You've..."

His hand like a greedy animal, he touched the boy's arms and legs. *Ik-su, your dad's just dreamed of hugging you.* He was already touching his backside and then groping around for his *gochu*.[2] The boy drew back.

"Dad, people can see."

"Oh kiddo, there's nothing wrong with a father touching his own son's *gochu*."

The boy smiled shyly, his face red like a ripe persimmon.

"I tried to get here fast, Dad, but the bus took forever."

"You're not late yet, are you?"

소년은 연시 같은 얼굴로 수줍게 웃었다.

"아빠, 빨리 오려고 했는데 버스가 자꾸 늑장을 부리 잖아."

"아직도 늦지 않았는데?"

그는 몸을 일으켜 아들의 고수머리를 손바닥으로 비 볐다.

"아빠보다 먼저 와 있으려고 했거든."

"그래도 소용없을걸?"

그는 완고한 할아버지처럼 말했다. 그러자 아들이 조 금 긴장하는 눈치였다.

"무슨 말이야?"

"아빠도 익수보다 먼저 도착하려고 딱 마음먹었단 말 이지."

비로소 아들의 얼굴에 긴장이 걷혔다.

"내가 보고 싶었어?"

"어디, 보고 싶었다 뿐이겠느냐?"

그는 가방을 추스르고 아들의 손을 잡았다.

"감독이 안 보내준 거야?"

아들이 재우쳐 물었다.

The man straightened up and patted the boy's curly head of hair.

"I wanted to be here before you."

"No use in that." The man spoke like a stubborn granddad, and the boy looked a little apprehensive.

"What do you mean?"

"I mean that *I* made up *my* mind to get here before *you* did."

The boy's face relaxed. "Because you missed me?"

"Words can't describe how much." He pushed up the strap of the bag and took his son's hand.

"But the supervisor wouldn't let you go?" the boy continued.

"Huh?"

"I mean, he wouldn't let you leave Saudi."

"Nope, he wouldn't." The man answered absent-mindedly, pulling his son along. The boy stood firm for a moment, resisting. The man looked at him in surprise and the boy laughed as if he had just been kidding.

"I heard it's really hot in Saudi Arabia, Dad," said the boy, swinging the man's arm vigorously.

"Yes."

"It was very cold here last winter."

"응?"

"사우디에서 말야?"

"그래."

그는 대충 대답을 하고 아들의 손을 끌었다. 소년은 안 끌려가려고 잠깐 발을 뻗디뎠다. 그가 놀란 눈으로 소년을 바라보자 소년은 장난이라는 듯 곧 헤헤 웃었다.

"아빠, 사우딘 무척 덥다며?"

아들이 그의 손을 힘껏 흔들며 말했다.

"덥지."

"지난겨울 여긴 굉장히 추웠어."

"나도 걱정했단다. 옷이라도 사 보내고 싶었지만……."

"알고 있어."

"뭘 말이냐?"

그가 얼른 되받아 물었다.

"거긴 겨울옷이 없잖아."

"이 녀석 아는 것도 많구나."

그는 아들의 궁둥이를 철썩 갈겼다.

"Yes, I was worried about it. I wanted to send some clothes or something, but..."

"I know."

"What do you mean by that?" the man asked quickly.

"There's no winter clothing there."

"You know all sorts of things." The man swatted him on the backside.

"No matter how cold it got, I could stand it. You were slaving away in a hot country..."

The man wanted to say something, but he couldn't think of the right words.

They came up from the underpass, and the enormous Kyobo Building was in front of them, blocking the horizon.

"This sure is a tall building, isn't it, Dad?" the boy said, looking at it stretching far up into the sky.

"Yeah."

"You build these kind of buildings in Saudi, right?"

"Who told you that?"

"Mom did. She said even before you went to Saudi, you built fine houses and tall apartments. So you'll make a nice house for us, too, someday."

"When did she say that?"

"아무리 추워도 꾹꾹 참았어. 아빠 더운 나라에서 고생하시는데……."

그는 뭐라고 말해 주고 싶었지만 무슨 말을 해야 좋을지 알 수 없었다.

그들은 지하도를 빠져나왔다. 거대한 '교보' 건물이 그들 앞을 가로막았다.

"아빠, 이 건물 참 높으다 그치?"

아들은 까마득한 건물을 올려다보며 말했다.

"그렇구나."

"아빠도 사우디서 이런 건물 짓는다며?"

"누가 그러데?"

"엄마가 그러던데? 사우디 가기 전에도 아빠 근사한 주택과 고층 아파트도 지었다고. 그래서 이담에 우리 집도 예쁘게 지을 거라고."

"엄마가 언제?"

"전에."

그래, 집을 짓는 일이라면 안 해본 게 없단다. 처음엔 골재 등짐을 지고 사오 층까지 비계다리를 오르내리기도 했지. 기소도 파고 콘크리트도 치면서 그렇게 뼈가

"Oh, a while ago."

Yes, when it comes to building houses, there's nothing I haven't done. In the beginning I went up and down the scaffolding ladder, taking loads of gravel to the fourth and fifth floors. I got pretty tough digging foundations and laying concrete. Eventually I built up my resume and was working at a construction company when I met your mother. At that time, even if my future wasn't a super highway rolling in front of me, it was a small, well-defined path. I wasn't a project manager, but I could have been if I wanted. And if you have a house, how hard can it be to live a happy life with a wife and kids? By the sweat of my brow, I managed to put down a large deposit on a little place when you came along. My one dream was to be a good dad...

They got on the bus, the boy in front. Even as they rode along, the boy didn't stop chattering. He told stories about school and about the kids in his class... He started one about his pregnant teacher.

"Dad, listen to this. There's this kid called Yeong-su who was fooling around during class and got in trouble with the teacher. And you know what? He was standing beside the podium with his arms in the air as punishment when he looked at the teacher's round belly. And you know what he said?"

굵었단다. 그러다가 제법 이력이 붙어 건설회사 소속으로 일할 때 네 엄마를 만났지. 그때만 해도 내 앞날은 툭 터진 대로는 아니라 해도 잘 닦인 소로쯤은 되었단다. 까짓것 현장 총감독쯤이야 언제 해먹어도 해먹을 것이고 집칸이나 지니면 처자식과 더불어 오순도순 사는 게 뭐가 그리 어렵겠니. 밑천이라고 해야 튼튼한 육신뿐이지만, 그래도 네가 생겼을 땐 작은 전세방도 얻고 살았단다. 내 꿈이 더도 말고 좋은 아빠가 되는 것이었는데…….

그는 아들을 앞세우고 버스에 올랐다. 아이는 버스를 타고도 끊임없이 재잘거렸다. 학교 이야기, 반 친구들 이야기…… 그리고 임신한 여선생 이야기를 시작했다.

"아빠, 있지. 영수란 애가 공부시간에 장난을 치다가 선생님한테 벌을 받았어. 근데 있지? 교탁 옆에서 두 팔을 들고 있다가 갑자기 선생님의 둥그런 배를 노려보는 거야. 그리고 뭐라고 말했는지 알아?"

"글쎄."

"너 이 자식, 그 뱃속에서 나오기만 해봐라. 내가 가만둘 줄 아니? 이러는 거야."

"What?"

"'You little bastard. Just watch yourself when you get out of the womb. I'll be waiting!'"

"Ha. That's no ordinary kid."

"And do you know what the teacher said back?"

"What?"

"She said, 'Yeong-su, you're forgiven. But when the baby comes out, you leave him alone. Got it?'"

The man laughed right out loud. With a quick wit like that, the woman would surely be a good teacher for Ik-su, too. He was pleased and re-lieved. What's more, the boy could tell a decent story! *You crazy kid, I wonder what you'll be when you grow up.* For Ik-su's first birthday celebration, they'd had a spool of thread, a pen and a candle set out for him to crawl around and grab, and he picked the candle first. His mother clapped her hands to-gether, saying it meant he'd be President for sure. He whisked the boy into his arms.

"You just grow up to be big and healthy," he said.

The man encircled his son's midsection with his arm and pulled him close, murmuring in his ear, "If a kid's a good talker, he'll become a lawyer. Every-one says so. Maybe you'll be a lawyer, too. But in

"하하, 그 녀석 보통이 아니구나."

"그랬더니 선생님이 어쩌셨는지 알아?"

"어쩌셨는데?"

"얘 영수야, 용서해줄게. 그럼, 선생님 뱃속에서 아기가 나왔을 때 너도 가만둬 줄래? 이러시는 거야."

그는 큰소리로 껄껄 웃었다. 그렇게 재치가 있다면 익수에게도 분명 좋은 선생이리라 싶었다. 그건 기분 좋으면서도 안심되는 일이었다. 게다가 아들놈은 조리 있게 얘기를 전달하는 법도 알고 있었다. 이 녀석은 커서 뭐가 될까. 돌 실타래와 연필과 양초를 두고 기어가 잡게 했을 때 아이는 먼저 양초를 집어들었다. 아내는 손뼉을 치며 틀림없이 대통령이 될 거라고 장담을 했고, 그는 아들을 번쩍 안아들고 말했다. 튼튼하게만 자라거라……. 그는 소년의 갈비뼈로 손을 넣고 꽉 당겨 안으며 속으로 중얼거렸다. 흔히들 말하지. 말 잘하면 변호사가 될 거라고. 너도 변호사가 될지도 모르겠구나. 그렇다면 아들아, 너랑 네 가정과 사회를 건강하게 하는 그런 변호사가 되려무나.

버스가 대공원 앞에 세워졌다. 부자는 손을 꼭 잡고

that case, I only hope you're the kind of lawyer that makes your family and society strong."

The bus stopped in front of the park. Father and son got off, holding hands tightly. Perhaps because it was Sunday, there were a lot of people in line for tickets. The man glanced back. Single cigarettes were on sale at the newspaper stand. Should he buy one? He put the thought out of his mind and squeezed Ik-su's hand.

The park was crowded with people: young couples with toddlers in tow, small kids getting pulled along by their grandmothers, children gathered in front of a balloon seller... The man felt dizzy for a moment, but quickly collected himself.

"Would you like a balloon?" he asked the boy, who was looking around wide-eyed.

"Dad, I'm not a little kid anymore."

"Then how about some cotton candy?"

"If you eat sweets your teeth will go bad."

"The ones your daddy buys for you will be all right."

He pulled his son over to the cotton candy seller, who was pouring a continuous stream of white sugar into a machine that whirled round and round. The man inadvertently looked inside. Each grain of

버스에서 내렸다. 일요일이어서 그런지 표를 사기 위해 줄을 선 사람들이 많았다. 그는 얼핏 뒤를 돌아보았다. 거기 신문좌판에 낱담배를 팔고 있었다. 한 개비만 살까……. 그는 그만두고 아들의 손을 잡아 쥐었다.

대공원 안은 사람들로 붐볐다. 어린애를 데리고 나온 젊은 부부들, 할머니 손에 끌려가는 꼬마, 풍선 장수 앞에 몰려 있는 아이들……. 그는 잠깐 현기증을 느꼈지만 재빨리 마음을 가다듬었다.

"풍선 하나 사줄까?"

사방을 두리번거리는 아들에게 그가 물었다.

"아빠두 참, 내가 어린애야?"

"그럼, 솜사탕은 어떠냐?"

"단것 먹으면 이빨이 썩는대."

"아빠가 사주는 건 괜찮을 거야."

그는 솜사탕 장수 앞으로 아들의 손을 끌었다. 들들들 돌아가는 기계 속으로 장사꾼은 연신 하얀 설탕을 넣었다. 그는 무심코 그 안을 들여다보았다. 설탕의 입자가 하얀 거미줄로 분해되면서 위로 떠오르고 있었다. 어느 양심수가 하던 얘기가 생각났다. 원심분리기 알죠? 제

sugar was being pulled into a white web-like thread that rose upwards. A story a political prisoner had once told him came to mind.

"Are you familiar with a centrifuge? It doesn't matter if you have nerves of steel, you turn pale if you're told you're going into a centrifuge. Once you're inside, you lose all semblance of human form, torn apart at high-speed rotation. And what's left is neither blood nor bone, only a few drops of water. Of course I have no way of knowing if they really use that kind of machine or not."

Prison was like a Nanji Island[3] for stories. Every odd story bandied about in society was delivered there like trash, and inmates wiled away their time sifting through it. He frowned. He shouldn't be thinking about that when he was on the outside, and worse, in front of his son! He took a glob of cotton candy from the vendor and handed it to the boy.

"Dad, look at the deer."

The boy led him over to the deer pen. The mother deer was licking the baby's hindquarters. Seeing this, the man felt a sudden urge, and whisked the boy up onto his shoulders.

"No. I'm too heavy."

아무리 담력이 강철인 사람두요, 원심분리기에 넣겠다고 하면 얼굴이 샛노래진대요. 일단 거기 들어가면 고도의 회전에 의해 사람은 형체도 없어진다나요. 남는 건 피나 뼈가 아니라 오직 몇 방울의 물뿐이랍니다. 아, 물론 실제 그런 게 사용되고 있는지 어떤지는 확인한 바 없지만 말입니다……. 교도소는 마치 이야기의 난지도 같은 곳이다. 사회인들이 뱉어낸 오만가지 이야기들이 쓰레기처럼 실려 오는 곳, 재소자들은 그 허섭스레기를 뒤져 그날의 시간을 요리한다. 그는 얼굴을 찌푸렸다. 밖에 나와서까지 그곳 생각을 하다니. 더욱이 아들놈 앞에서. 그는 장사꾼이 뭉쳐준 솜사탕을 받아 아들에게 쥐어주었다.

"아빠, 저기 사슴 좀 봐."

소년이 사슴 방목장으로 그를 이끌었다. 어미사슴이 새끼의 엉덩이를 핥아주고 있었다. 그 모습을 보자 그도 참을 수가 없었던지 아들을 번쩍 들어 올려 목말을 태웠다.

"싫어. 난 무겁단 말야."

"시멘트 부대 하나보다 가벼운데?"

"You're lighter than a sack of cement."

"Really?" the boy asked right in the man's ear.

"Yep."

To reassure him, the man held each of his son's hands in the air and danced a little as he walked. Then the sweetness of something made his heart overflow with happiness. It was the feel of his son's *gochu* lying soft against the back of his neck.

"Dad, let me down." The boy spoke anxiously, but the man just smiled. He didn't know why the feel of his son's *gochu* made him so happy, but he continued his carefree smiling and prancing.

"Look Dad, there's a train. Let's go ride it."

"Where would you like that train to take you, Little Lord?" he said, adopting the persona of a traditional mask dance character, sounding eager to please.[4]

"Dad's country!" the boy replied instantly.

"And what do you intend to do in your father's land?"

"I want us to live together. Let's go!"

Live together… The words struck him in the ribs like an arrow coming flying out of nowhere. Even so, he moved his shoulders in time to an unheard rhythm as he walked.

"정말?"

소년이 그의 귀에 입을 바짝 대고 물었다.

"그렇대두."

그는 무겁지 않다는 걸 보이기 위해 아이의 두 손을 잡고 둥개춤을 추며 걸었다. 그때 달콤한 그 무엇이 가슴속으로 찰랑찰랑 넘쳐왔다. 그것의 정체는 목덜미 뒤를 부드럽게 누르는 아이의 고추였다.

"아빠, 그만 내릴게."

소년이 걱정스럽게 말했으나 그는 그저 싱글벙글 웃었다. 자식 놈 고추의 느낌이 왜 그렇게 기분이 좋은지는 알 수 없었지만 그는 연신 웃으며 겅중겅중 뛰고 있었다.

"아빠, 저기 땡땡이 기차 있다. 우리 그것 타자."

"땡땡이 기차를 타고 어딜 가시렵니까, 도련님?"

그가 취바리 흉내로 비나리를 치자, 소년이 얼른 되받았다.

"아빠의 나라로!"

"아빠의 나라에 가서 무얼 하시렵니까?"

"함께 살려고 그런다. 어서 가자!"

"Very well, Little Lord. Let's go."

They rode the train and the Ferris wheel together, and took in the House of Magic.

"Now, shall I check Ik-su's belly clock to find out how hungry he is?"

He put his ear up to the child's stomach.

"Belly clock?" The boy giggled, amused by the expression.

"Good grief! There's a growling signal from your stomach that means 'send food right away.'"

"Does your belly clock say you're hungry too?"

"Yes. Let's go up that hill and have lunch."

"You packed some food along?"

"Yes. You like doughnuts, don't you? I brought some boiled eggs as well."

The man staked out a grassy spot on a hill away from the foot traffic. Opening his bag, one by one he set out the *kimbap*, milk and everything else.

"Wow! So many different things!"

Ik-su snatched up a doughnut as if he were starving. The man opened the milk carton and passed it to the boy.

"Take your time eating or you'll get indigestion. And have some milk with your food."

"You eat too, Dad."

함께 살려고……. 그 말은 불시에 날아온 화살처럼 그의 갈비뼈를 쏘았다. 그래도 그는 어깨춤을 추면서 걷고 있었다.

"좋아요, 도련님. 어서 가시죠."

그는 아들과 함께 땡땡이 기차를 타고, 허니문카를 타고, '요술의 집'을 구경했다.

"자, 이제 우리 익수의 배시계가 얼마나 고픈지 귀 한 번 대볼까."

그는 아이의 배로 귀를 가져갔다.

"배시계?"

소년은 그 말이 재미난지 걀걀걀 웃어댔다.

"어이구, 뱃속에서 얼른 밥 들여보내라고 쪼르륵 신호를 보내는데?"

"아빠 배시계도 고파?"

"그래, 저기 동산에 가서 점심 먹자."

"점심 싸 왔어?"

"그럼, 너 도나스 좋아하지? 찐 계란도 있어."

그는 사람들이 한적한 동산으로 올라가 잔디 위에 자리를 잡았다. 그리고 가방을 열고 김밥과 우유 등 준비

The boy passed him a roll of *kimbap*. He took it, but didn't bite in; he just watched his son dreamily. *You're better than your old man,* he thought, recalling a scene from his childhood. He and his father had packed a lunch and had gone to weed a rice paddy on a steep mountainside. He kept picking a handful of weeds and looking up at the sun, picking a handful of weeds and looking up at the sun. He was looking forward to mealtime. Before the sun had even reached its peak, he broke down and called out, "Dad, let's have lunch."

"Come and eat then."

In the time it took him to rinse his feet off in the paddy water, his father had snapped some branches off of a bush and made chopsticks out of them. There was only one tin lunchbox. Overcome with hunger, however, he didn't care how many lunchboxes there were; he just took the lid off and began shoveling food into his mouth. His father took a bite, and then quietly laid down the chopsticks and walked over to the ditch. After every scrap of food was gone, the boy went to look for his father, and discovered him pushing through the grass, biting the leaves off of a mile-a-minute weed.

"Dad, what are you doing?"

해 온 것들을 하나하나 꺼내 놓았다.

"야! 별난 거 별난 거 다 있구나."

소년은 시장했던지 급히 도넛을 집었다. 그는 우유를
따서 아들 손에 들려 주었다.

"체할라, 천천히 먹어라. 우유도 마시면서."

"아빠도 먹어."

소년은 김밥 하나를 집어주었다. 그는 그것을 받아 한
입 베물다 말고 아들을 물끄러미 바라보았다. 넌 그래
도 이 아비보다 낫구나. 그는 자신이 어렸을 때의 일을
떠올렸다. 아버지와 함께 밥을 싸들고 산비탈에 있는
천수답 논에 피를 뽑으러 갔을 때였다. 그는 피 한 줌 뽑
고 해를 보고 또 한 줌 뽑고 해를 보곤 했었다. 얼른 밥
이 먹고 싶었던 것이다. 해가 머리꼭대기에 오기도 전
에 그는 마침내 소리치고 말았다.

"아부지 점심 묵읍시더."

"오냐, 묵자."

그가 논물로 발을 씻는 사이 아버지는 싸릿대를 꺾어
젓가락을 만들어왔다. 한데 도시락은 하나였다. 그는
도시락이야 몇 개든 간에 급히 뚜껑을 열고 밥을 퍼먹

His father wiped his mouth quickly and held out a handful of ripe red raspberries. "Come and try some of these."

Ik-su spoke. "Dad, are you okay?"

"Yes. I just thought of something your grandfather used to say."

"What did Grandpa say?"

"He used to say it all the time. The best things in this world are..."

"What?"

"The best things are food in your son's mouth, and water on the rice paddies."

"That's right. A boy needs to eat a lot to get big and a paddy needs a lot of water for the plants to produce lots of seed heads."

"You little devil. I see there's nothing you don't know."

The man took a handful of the boy's curly hair, giving him a friendly shake. The boy broke into a smile, and he pulled the man's hand down and began stroking it gingerly.

"Dad, I was worried what would happen if I didn't recognize you," he said softly.

Yes, the man had been surprised when Ik-su

기 시작했다. 아버지는 한 젓가락을 뜨고는 슬그머니 손을 놓고 도랑 저쪽으로 갔다. 그가 도시락을 말끔히 비우고 아버지를 찾았을 때 아버지는 풀더미를 헤치고 며느리배꼽 잎을 훑어 먹고 있었다.

"아부지 뭐 하닝겨?"

그러자 아버진 얼른 입술을 닦은 뒤 한 손을 내밀었다.

"옹냐, 이거 묵어라."

그건 빨갛게 익은 멍덕딸기였다.

"아빠, 왜 그러구 있어?"

소년이 물었다.

"응, 할아버지가 하시던 말씀을 생각했다."

"할아버지가 뭐라셨는데?"

"네 할아버진 늘 말씀하셨단다. 이 세상에서 가장 좋은 게 뭐냐……."

"그게 뭔데?"

"그건 말이다. 아들 입에 밥 들어가는 것과 논에 물 들어가는 거라고……."

"그야 그렇겠지. 아들은 밥을 많이 먹어야 얼른 자라

called out "Dad." How had the boy recognized the face of a father who'd been absent since he was four?

"I brought a picture just in case, but I knew it was you right away even without looking at it. I'm not saying you don't look a little different, though."

The boy pulled the photo out of his jacket pocket and showed it to him. It was a family picture taken at Ik-su's first birthday party, showing the man and his wife, with the boy between them.

"Do you want to keep it?" The boy asked, after the man had stared at the photo for a long time.

"No. It's your picture."

For a moment, all he could see was his wife's face. The last time she'd visited was four years ago. That day she'd just sat there for two minutes with her head hanging down, not saying anything. Of course he wasn't able to talk either. He was afraid that when she expressed the thoughts pent up inside her, they'd be like live explosives.

Eventually she said, as if sighing, "The boy is starting school."

These were her only words. The man had wanted very badly to hold her hand. The inmates all said they longed for the bodies of their wives even

고 논에는 물이 잘 들어가야 벼가 많이 열리니까."

"이 녀석, 너 정말 모르는 게 없구나."

그는 아들의 고수머리를 잡아 흔들었다. 아들은 배시
시 웃으며 그의 손을 끌어내려 가만가만 만지기 시작했
다.

"아빠, 난 아빠를 몰라보면 어쩌나 걱정했었어."

소년이 나직한 목소리로 말했다. 그래, 나도 네가 아
빠라고 불렀을 때 무척 놀랐단다. 만 네 살 때 헤어진 아
빠의 얼굴을 어떻게 알아보았을까……

"혹시나 해서 사진을 들고 왔지만 사진 안 봐도 금방
알아보겠던데? 어딘가 좀 달라 보이기도 했지만 말야."

그리고 소년은 혹시나 해서 들고 왔다는 사진을 잠바
주머니에서 꺼내 보였다. 그 사진은 익수가 돌 때 아이
를 가운데 하고 아내와 함께 찍은 가족 사진이었다.

"아빠 가질래?"

그가 한참 동안 사진을 보고 있자 소년이 말했다.

"아니다. 이건 니 사진이잖니."

아내의 얼굴이 망막 가득 떠올랐다. 그녀가 마지막으
로 면회 온 것은 사 년 전이었다. 그날 아내는 이 분이

more than they missed their children. Wouldn't that be true for anyone? Visiting time was up. His wife was the first to turn to leave.

"Go see my sister. She'll buy Ik-su a book bag and some notebooks," he said in desperation to his wife's turned back.

She paused briefly and then just continued on out. In the letter he received a few days later, she announced she'd given up their son. *I don't believe I can raise a child on my own. Whether I start work at a factory or as a housekeeper again, I can't take him along... And your sister has hardly enough money to get by. I can't bring myself to leave him with her. So I'm going to have to give him up for the time being. He's at the address below.* She'd written the contact information for an orphanage.

Ik-su had been an orphan for four years. The man had worried so much about him over this time, and here he'd grown into a fine young boy! How many nights had he lain sleepless on account of his child? At the sound of the rain dripping into the gutter, he saw Ik-su eating cold maize gruel, and if it snowed, he dreamed that Ik-su was freezing to death. He looked out into empty space. For a long time at first, he'd resented his wife as well.

지나도록 아무 말도 없이 고개를 떨구고 있었다. 그 역시 입을 열지 못했다. 아내 마음속에 갇혀 있는 생각들이 입 밖으로 나오기만 하면 어떤 폭발물이 될 것 같아 그는 두려웠다. 이윽고 아내가 한숨처럼 말했다.

"아이가 입학을 해요."

그 말뿐이었다. 그때 그는 몹시 아내의 손이 잡고 싶었다. 재소자들은 누구나가 말한다. 가장 절실한 건 새끼보다 마누라 궁둥이지. 그건 누구라 해도 마찬가질걸? 면회 시간이 끝났다. 아내가 그보다 먼저 돌아섰다. 그때 그는 아내의 등에다 대고 다급하게 말했었다.

"누님한테 가봐. 익수 책가방과 공책을 사주실 거야."

아내는 잠깐 멈추었다가 그대로 나가버렸다. 그리고 며칠 후 도착한 편지엔 자식 놈과의 이별을 고하고 있었다. 난 아이를 혼자 맡을 자신이 없어요. 공장에 취직을 하든 다시 식모살이를 시작하든 아이를 데리고는……. 그렇다고 넉넉하게 살지도 못하는 당신 누님에게는 차마 맡길 수가 없구요. 그래서 당분간 익수를 떼놓기로 했어요. 아래 주소가 그 애 있는 곳이에요……. 아내가 적어 보낸 주소는 고아원이었다.

He thought he'd kill her just as soon as he got out.

Gradually, though, he started to forgive her. She was smarter than others, and she wanted the best for their son, but she'd spent ten years keeping house for a construction company manager. How could she be expected to raise and educate a child without any education or relatives to help her? At the orphanage, Ik-su would be able to study. Perhaps that was why she'd given him up when she loved him so much... But why hadn't she visited the prison after that? The man had transferred back up to Anyang penitentiary after moving down to Daegu for a while, so maybe she didn't know where he was. From the moment he met his son, he'd wanted to ask about her, but he stopped himself out of fear.

"Dad, I read your letter every day," the boy said, scooping eggshells into the empty milk carton. "You said you'd come back to Korea when the forsythias bloomed... but spring usually takes forever to come."

The man took a while to respond. "Yes, but the forsythias did bloom, didn't they?"

"When the next letter came, they still weren't out. And it was April. So I was really worried. Today,

익수가 고아가 된 지도 사 년……. 그렇게 염려했던 아들은 의젓한 소년으로 자랐다. 얼마나 많은 나날을 이놈 때문에 잠을 설쳤던가. 낙숫물 소리만 들려도 강냉이죽 먹는 모습을 상상했고, 눈만 내려도 얼어죽는 꿈을 꾸었었다. 그는 먼 허공을 바라보았다. 처음 얼마 동안은 아내를 원망도 했었다. 나가기만 하면 죽여버릴 테다.

그러나 그는 차츰 아내를 이해하기 시작했다. 남다르게 영리하고 샘이 많은 여자였지만 현장소장 집에서 십여 년간 남의집살이를 한 사람이었다. 학벌 없고 친척 없는 그녀가 혼자 무슨 능력으로 아이를 키우고 또 가르칠 것인가. 고아원에 가면 공부는 할 수 있다. 그래서 아내가 그렇게 사랑하던 아들을 고아원으로 보냈는지도 모른다……. 한데 그뒤 왜 한 번도 면회를 오지 않았을까. 대구로 갔다가 다시 안양 교도소로 이감했기 때문에 그녀가 주소를 모르는 것일까. 그는 아들을 만난 순간부터 아내의 소식을 묻고 싶었지만, 그럴 때마다 어떤 두려움이 그 욕구를 가로막았다.

"아빠, 난 매일 아빠 편지를 읽었어."

too, I was worried you might not come."

"I said I would, so why wouldn't I?"

"Then you won't go now?" the boy asked, looking at him intently.

"I told you in the letter. I'm just here on a break..."

The boy picked up the eggshells and put them back again. The movement was cautious but at the same time deliberate, like someone expertly printing with a firm hand. The man couldn't shake his irritation. If his wife hadn't said he'd gone abroad to earn money, he'd have been able to explain his position to the boy. That was the problem. He felt like firing off letters to the boy every day, expressing his care and concern, but his wife had taken that chance away from him. Was she aware that her silly talk had created a wall like this between them? When he heard that he could get a special day pass as a reward for seven years of good behavior, he'd managed to think of a way of sending mail by way of former inmates, and so twice he was able to get letters to his son. But even after inserting the words "Saudi" and "coming back to Korea" into his sentences, he'd felt frustrated, as if something was caught in his throat. Presently the boy picked up the empty milk carton and eggshells left over from

소년이 빈 우유통에다 계란 껍질을 주워 담으며 말했다.

"개나리가 필 때쯤 귀국하마……. 그런데 봄은 자꾸 늑장을 부리잖아."

"그래도 개나리는 피었잖니."

그가 한참 만에 아이의 말을 받았다.

"그 다음 편지를 받았을 때도 개나리는 눈도 틔우지 않았어. 사월인데……, 그래서 얼마나 걱정했는지 몰라. 오늘도 아빠가 안 오시면 어쩌나……."

"약속은 아빠가 했는데 왜 안 오겠냐?"

"그럼, 이제 안 가?"

소년이 그를 빤히 쳐다보며 물었다. 그는 슬그머니 시선을 떨구었다.

"편지에 썼잖니. 이번엔 휴가라고……."

소년은 다시 계란 껍질을 주워 담았다. 그 동작이 어떻게나 조심스럽던지 마치 또박또박 글을 쓰는 듯했다. 그는 자꾸만 성이 말랐다. 아내가 아빠는 외국으로 돈 벌러 갔다는 말만 하지 않았던들 그는 아들에게 자신의 입장을 설명했을 것이다. 어디 그뿐인가. 아들에게 걱

lunch and stood up.

"Dad, I'll just throw these away and come back."

"Okay. Hurry up."

The boy went down the hill. Weaving through the blossoming trees, he reached a trashcan by the pathway and deposited the garbage. Then he looked back up, and motioned that he'd be going somewhere farther down for a moment, probably the restroom. The man gazed wretchedly at the figure of his son hurrying away.

"You have until seven." The words of the prison warden rang in his ears. "Be just one hour late and you won't get the same privilege next year. Of course, you already know this." The man studied the sun. It was pushing through the clouds, traveling quickly. He checked the path below, but didn't see the boy. He looked at the sun again. It had the face of a clock, and the big and little hands were going around it at top speed. Three, four, five, six, seven o'clock... And suddenly everything was dark. Trembling, he turned over on the grass and lay on his stomach. *Time always betrays me*. Viewed from the squat toilet in his cell, the sun had been like a clock with no hands. He bit into his forearm. It was as if all of his thoughts were blades, filed to sharp

정과 사랑이 넘치는 편지를 매일매일 띄우고 싶었지만 그런 가능성마저도 아내는 애초부터 잘라놓고 말았다. 생각 없이 지껄인 말 한마디가 이렇게 벽을 만들고 있다는 걸 아내는 알고 있을까. 칠 년 모범수에 하루 특박(特泊)이 허용된다는 말을 들었을 때, 그는 간신히 출소자 인편을 생각해냈고 그래서 아들에게 두 번 편지를 보낼 수가 있었다. 그 편지를 쓰면서 귀국이란 말과 사우디란 말을 기입하고서도 뭐가 걸린 듯 가슴이 답답했었다. 이윽고, 소년이 김밥을 먹은 도시락 껍질과 빈 우유통을 들고 일어났다.

"아빠, 이것 버리고 올게."

"그래. 빨리 갔다오너라."

아들이 동산을 내려갔다. 꽃나무 사이로 가렸다 보였다 하면서 소년은 길가에 놓인 쓰레기통까지 가서 손에 든 것을 집어넣었다. 그리고 아이는 잠깐 동안 위를 올려다 보며 저 아래 갔다 오겠다는 손짓을 보냈다. 화장실에라도 가려는 모양이었다. 그는 바쁘게 내려가는 아들의 뒷모습을 무연히 바라보았다.

일곱 시까지야. 교도소 소장의 말이 이명으로 들려왔

points. He shook his head hard. He told himself that the next eight years would be nothing. They'd go by in an instant. Closing his eyes, he saw Seung-sik's face, pale in front of him.

The man and his friend Seung-sik had come up to Seoul from the same hometown. Seung-sik had got on at an electrical company and swore he'd become a first-class technician. One day, however, Seung-sik came to see him at an apartment construction site, saying he was out of work. That evening, the man bought some *soju*. As the alcohol took hold, Seung-sik grabbed his hand and stroked his rough, work-hardened flesh.

"You and I, we said we'd make it big, but we've come to Seoul and we work like slaves." Seung-sik's voice was thick with emotion.

"Working for the man is always like that," the man said quietly, as if to steady him.

At that, Seung-sik lost his temper. "We're selling our labor. We didn't agree to be slaves! The company I was fired from treated all its workers like we were machines or animals. If you were late just one minute, you were turned back at the gate, and you worked overtime every day, even Sundays. If you

다. 한 시간만 늦어도 내년 혜택에 지장이 있다구. 물론 자네야 알아서 할 사람이지만 말이네. 그는 해를 쳐다보았다. 해는 구름을 밀어내고 바쁘게 흘러갔다. 그는 얼른 길 아래쪽을 더듬어 보았다. 아들놈은 보이지 않았다. 그는 다시 해를 보았다. 해가 시계판으로 보이면서 작고 큰 바늘이 아주 빠른 속도로 돌아가고 있었다. 세 시, 네 시, 다섯 시, 여섯 시, 일곱 시……. 그리고 별안간 사방이 캄캄해졌다. 그는 진저리치듯 몸을 뒤집고 잔디밭에 엎드렸다. 시간은 항상 나를 배반해. 뺑끼통에서 내다보던 해는 바늘 없는 시계판이더니……. 그는 팔뚝을 이빨로 잘근잘근 깨물었다. 자칫 머릿속의 모든 생각들이 쭈뼛쭈뼛 날을 세울 것만 같았다. 그는 세차게 고개를 흔들었다. 앞으로 팔 년, 그건 잠깐이야, 잠깐……. 그는 눈을 감았다. 승식의 얼굴이 하얗게 떠올랐다.

승식은 함께 서울로 온 고향 친구였다. 전기 회사에 취직했을 때 반드시 일류기술자가 되겠다고 다짐하던 승식이 어느 날 실직했다면서 아파트 현장으로 그를 찾아왔다. 그날 저녁 그가 소주를 샀다. 술기운이 돌자 승

got burnt out and missed a weekend shift, or dozed off during the civil defense drill,[5)] then they had no pity. They fired you. What kind of place is that for a man to work?"

So Seung-sik said he'd form a union. At the first meeting, when members were airing different opinions on pay increases, bonuses, anti-discrimination policies and work leave, the company officials had descended on them with clubs.

"They just swung their clubs at us recklessly, telling us to break it up fast or we'd all be killed... It was savage. But we didn't back down. We tried to convince them, even as we lay there beaten and bleeding. A labor union isn't an instrument for picking fights, it's for legally restoring the rights and interests of both sides. But I'm telling you—no matter what we said, they refused to allow us to meet."

"Those idiots running the company, they thought that from the day we organized, we'd turn from workers into thieves, we'd clean out their pockets. How can they expect to produce cutting-edge products when they have such a low, miser-like mentality, believing workers are no better than animals or machines?"

식은 그의 손을 잡아당겨 딱딱해진 굳은살을 어루만졌다.

"너나 나나 출세하겠다고 서울까지 와서는 죽도록 노예 생활만 했구나."

그 목소리가 하도 비장해서 그는 조용히 타이르듯 말했다.

"남 밑에서 일한다는 게 다 그렇지 뭐."

그러자 승식이 결기를 세웠다.

"우리가 노동력을 판 것이지 노예가 되겠다고 한 건 아니잖아? 한데 내가 떨려난 그 회사는 근로자들이 전부 기계나 짐승인 줄 안단 말야. 단 일 분만 지각해도 수위실에서 되돌려 보내질 않나, 일요일도 없이 나날이 잔업이지, 어쩌다 몸살이 나서 휴일 근무에 빠져도, 민방위 시간에 졸아도 가차 없이 해고를 시켜버리니 이게 어디 사람이 일할 곳인가?"

그래서 승식은 노조를 결성했다는 것이다. 그리고 첫 모임을 열어 임금 인상·상여금·차별대우 폐지·휴가제 등 다양한 의견을 발표하고 있을 때 회사 간부들이 각자 몽둥이를 들고 들이닥쳤다고 했다.

"And also, even though unions are centered around workers' rights, they help keep companies stable too. And they help with social development. But the higher-ups in their greed—they don't know that. What they finally came up with was no more than another ploy—they called me in to say they'd offer me a promotion or a large raise if I broke up the union, and fast. So I told the director of general affairs, 'Sir, we aren't going to be demanding little nuisances, getting in everyone's way, and we're not asking to take over the company. All we want is for both sides to get a square deal. That way the workers can live like human beings and the company can survive into the future.' So I was advised to quit; actually, I was forced out."

Seung-sik added that he'd written a letter to union headquarters and had filed a complaint with the labor ministry. Then he went on to down two more shots, one after the next.

"Has anyone in your position ever won?" the man asked cautiously.

"Yes. There's the case of the chemical workers' union at J Pharmaceuticals. From what I heard, even that company didn't stand for unions in the beginning. If members demonstrated against union

"닥치는 대로 몽둥이를 휘두르면서, 빨리 해산 안 하면 다 죽이겠다는데……, 참 살벌했었지. 그래도 우린 물러나지 않았어. 얻어맞아 피를 흘리면서도 그들을 설득해보았지. 노조가 쟁의만을 위한 수단이 아니라 합법적으로 서로의 권익을 회복하자는 것이다……. 하지만 말야, 아무리 설명을 해도 회사에서는 절대 노조를 허용하지 않겠다는 거야. 얼간이 같은 고용주들이 글쎄, 노조가 결성되면 그날부터 근로자들이 자기 주머니를 털어 먹는 강도로 변하는 줄 안다니까. 그저 근로자란 기계나 짐승이 되어야 한다고 생각하는 그런 놀부 심보로 무슨 창의적인 제품이 생산되겠어? 사실 노조란 노동자의 권익도 있지만, 그와 더불어 회사의 안정과 사회의 발전이 도모되거든. 한데 그 지폐대가리들은 몰라. 기껏 머리 쓴다는 게 날 불러다 승진은 물론, 월급도 듬뿍 올려줄 테니 노조를 빨리 해산시키라는 회유책이니……. 그래 내가 말했지. 총무부장님, 이건 우리가 뭐 중뿔난 도깨비가 되겠다거나 상전 노릇을 하자는 게 아니잖습니까? 서로 정당하자는 것뿐입니다. 그래야 근로자도 살고 회사도 살죠. 그랬더니 권고사직을, 아니

54

suppression, the other employees threatened them, assaulted them, and went so far as to stab them in the eyes... But you know what? In the end, even the pigheaded company founder saw reason. Now, if anything, I've heard that the company actively supports labor."

The man had never worked at an office, and he couldn't understand everything Seung-sik said. But he knew one thing for sure: Seung-sik was right-minded, and wouldn't get himself involved in useless schemes. Then the man's first priority would have to be his friend's livelihood.

Filling Seung-sik's empty glass, he asked, "That may be, but from now on, how are you going to make a living?"

"I have no other choice. Until the matter is resolved, I'll have to get on as a laborer or something."

Seung-sik made light of the situation, but the man's thoughts turned to his friend's young daughter. Whatever higher purpose you serve, your duty to your family comes first. So he recommended Seung-sik take a job as a day laborer, and referred him to the supervisor the next day. He only learned about it later, but the supervisor set the condition

지, 더 정확히 말해서 강제 퇴직을 당한 거야."

그리고 승식은 노동청에다 고발하고 노조본부에 진정을 냈다고 덧붙인 다음 거푸 두 잔의 술을 비웠다.

"자네 같은 일을 한 사람들이 이긴 사례도 있나?"

그가 조심스럽게 물었다.

"있지. ㅈ제약 회사 화학노조가 그 케이슨데, 그 이름난 제약 회사에서도 초창기 땐 탄압이 지독했다더군. 노조 탄압을 중지하라고 조합원들이 농성을 하면 직원들이 공갈을 치고 집단구타를 하고, 그것도 모자라 눈을 찌르고…… 그랬지만 말야, 결국 그 옹고집 설립자도 자신의 무지를 깨달았다나. 지금은 오히려 적극적으로 후원한다더라."

그는 회사에 다녀보지 않아서 승식의 말을 다 이해하지는 못했다. 그러나 올곧은 승식이가 허튼 일을 저지르고 다닐 성품이 아니란 것만은 잘 알고 있었다. 그래서 무엇보다도 먼저 그 친구의 생활 걱정이 앞섰는지도 모른다.

그는 빈 잔에 술을 채우며 물었다.

"그나저나 앞으로 생활은 어쩔 참인가?"

that ten percent would be deducted from Seung-sik's daily wages. At any rate, his friend became a day worker, responsible for taking loads of gravel up the scaffolding.

About a month passed in this way. Seung-sik, anxiously waiting to hear back from the labor ministry, met his death one day, but as a construction worker, not as a technician. He fell from the third floor. The police concluded that he'd slipped. The man was incredulous. Anyway, it was strange that he'd fallen from the third floor and not the scaffolding ladder. He went to find the other men on Seung-sik's crew.

"That guy. Yesterday, too, he was meaning to have it out with the supervisor..."

"Have it out about what?"

"Really? You depend on this company for your livelihood, and you don't have any idea what's going on here? At first, the supervisor promised that when this job was done, he'd keep us on when he moved on to the next project, building apartments in Gangnam."

Everyone at the materials management cafeteria knew about this, too.

"So?"

"별수 없잖아. 그 일이 해결날 때까진 날품이라도 팔아야지."

승식은 매우 자조적이었지만 그는 녀석의 어린 딸을 생각했다. 뜻이야 어떻든 우선 가족들 생계는 해결해야 한다. 그래서 그는 잡역부라도 할 것을 권했고 다음 날 현장감독에게 승식을 부탁했다. 한데 나중에 안 일이지만 현장감독은 승식에게 일당 중에서 일 할을 떼기로 한 조건을 내세웠다는 것이다. 어쨌거나 녀석은 잡역부가 되어 자갈질통을 지고 비계를 오르내렸다.

그렇게 한 달쯤 되어 가던 어느 날이었다. 노동청으로부터 연락오기를 애타게 기다리던 승식은 기술자로서가 아니라 공사장 노무자로 죽고 말았다. 삼 층에서 추락한 것이었다. 경찰은 실족사로 단정했다. 그는 믿을 수가 없었다. 게다가 비계다리도 아닌 삼 층에서 떨어졌다는 게 아무래도 이상했다. 그는 승식과 한조로 일하던 인부들을 찾아갔다.

"어제도 그 사람은 감독한테 따지겠다고 벼르더니만……."

"뭘 따져요?"

"To put it bluntly, we were quietly giving up ten per cent of our wages to him as a bribe to stay on. But the plan didn't work out. The supervisor said that orders from above required him to hire future work crews through a foreman subcontractor,[6] and obviously he couldn't make good on his promise. So anyone unhappy with the situation was encouraged to quit right away."

There was the problem. Knowing Seung-sik, he wouldn't have been able to stand for this, and things might have gotten ugly when he confronted the supervisor about it. And didn't the supervisor have his living quarters on the third floor? The man called the manager to find out about the new subcontracting system. The manager denied ordering any such thing. Now the man was making headway. The man's wife had been keeping house for the manager for a long time, so the manager had no reason to lie to him.

Around dinnertime, he took a shovel and went up to the third floor. First, he inspected the area. On the far right side, construction of the wall and balcony was going on, but on the side where the supervisor's makeshift quarters had been built from panels, there was only a pillar and the floor. There was a good

"허, 이 사람도 이 회사에 명줄 걸려 있다고 소식이 깡통일세. 애초에 감독이 약속하기를 이번 공사 끝나고 강남 쪽 맨션으로 넘어갈 그때도 인부 교체는 않겠다고 했지."

그건 자재관리 함바[飯場]에서도 다 알고 있는 사실이다.

"그래서요?"

"막말로 그래서 우리가 잠자코 일 할을 상납한 게 아닌가. 아, 그런데 그게 틀어졌다는 게야. 십장 도급제로 넘기라는 상부 지시가 있어서 부득이 그 약속을 이행할 수 없다더군. 그러면서 그게 못마땅한 사람은 당장 그만두어도 좋다나, 허 참……."

문제는 거기에 있었다. 승식이 성질에 그걸 참을 수 없었을 것이고, 그래서 감독한테 따지다가 변을 당했을지도 모른다. 더욱이 현장감독의 임시 막사 또한 그 삼층에 있지 않은가. 그는 소장에게 전화를 걸어 십장도급제에 대해 알아보았다. 그런 걸 지시한 사실이 없다는 것이었다. 이제 실마리가 잡혔다. 오래도록 아내를 데리고 있었던 소장이 그에게 있는 사실을 없다고 말할

chance Seung-sik had walked backwards here and fallen off the edge. The man stood the shovel against a panel and called to the supervisor.

"What, is there some problem with the materials?"

The supervisor knew the man was Seung-sik's friend, but he was playing dumb.

"Why did you try to trick Seung-sik?"

Asked point blank like this, the supervisor turned pale. "It wasn't just him, it was all of the laborers."

"From what I understand, it was your idea."

"What?"

"You said you had orders from above to hire crews through a subcontractor, but I found out the manager didn't know anything about it."

"It's public knowledge now, so I'll be honest with you. Your friend was an agitator. As you know, we've got close to two hundred workers here. Suppose he started stirring up trouble, like he did at his old workplace. Who do you think would be held responsible for the results of all of that?"

"So the company told you to make the first move and get rid of him?"

"You asshole. Are you trying to set me up?"

"If not, then what happened on the third floor to make him fall?"

리도 없었다.

그는 저녁 무렵 삽을 챙겨들고 삼 층으로 올라갔다. 그리고 먼저 주위를 살폈다. 오른편 저쪽에서 벽과 베란다 공사를 해오고 있었지만 패널로 세워 만든 감독 막사 이쪽엔 바닥과 기둥뿐이었다. 승식은 바로 여기서 뒷걸음치다가 실족했을 가능성이 컸다. 그는 막사 옆에 삽을 세워두고 감독을 불러냈다.

"왜, 자재 착오라도 생겼나?"

승식과 친구란 걸 잘 알면서도 감독이 시침을 뗐다.

"승식이 왜 물먹이려 했소?"

그가 단도직입적으로 묻자 감독의 안색이 싹 달라졌다.

"그건 그 사람뿐만 아니라 전 잡역부들을……."

"그게 바로 당신 착상이라던데?"

"무슨 소린가?"

"당신은 상부의 지시라고 했다지만, 상부에서는 그런 사실조차도 모르고 있던데?"

"다 아는 처지니까 사실대로 말하지. 그 친군 불순분자야. 자네도 알다시피 여긴 이백 명 가까운 잡역부들

"He came up to argue with me. He knew that we were changing our hiring policy and replacing the crew because of him. But he still thought it was unfair and he was going to report me. He was talking a load of crap."

"Seung-sik would have said one more thing. You lured workers with your promises and skimmed the tops off their wages."

"I did not!" The supervisor turned red.

"And he'd have said, either tell everything to the manager or prepare for charges of double dealing. So you were trapped. To get out of it, you had to kill him!"

The man snatched up the shovel and walked right up to the supervisor. The supervisor drew back, trembling like a seed leaf.

"I didn't use a shovel."

In the confusion of the moment, the supervisor confessed.

"It was like this. I approached step by step, just like you're doing. Then he wasn't watching behind him, so he drifted back and lost his footing."

The man brandished the shovel and moved closer.

"No. I..."

"Yes, of course. You could have eliminated that

이 있어. 한데 전에 있던 회사에서처럼 인부들을 쑤석거려 봐. 그럼, 그 사후대책은 누가 책임지지?"

"그래서 회사에서 먼저 승식을 없애달라고 했소?"

"아니, 이 자식이 누굴 잡으려고 그런 터무니없는 모함을!"

"그게 아니라면 어째서 삼 층에서 그런 일이 일어났단 말이오!"

"그 자식이 따지러 왔더군. 도급젠가 뭔가로 인부 교체한다는 것이 자기 때문임을 안다. 그렇다 해도 그건 부당하니까 고발하겠다⋯⋯. 원, 말 같은 소릴 해야지."

"승식이가 말한 게 또 있을 텐데 당신은 교묘한 미끼로 인부들의 노임을 뜯어 먹고⋯⋯."

"난 그런 사실 없어!"

감독이 재빨리 부인했다.

"그리고 승식은 말했어. 그 모든 사실을 사장께 알리든가 아니면 사기로 고발하겠노라고. 그래서 당신은 궁지에 몰린 거야. 그 궁지를 모면하자면 승식을 죽여야만 했어!"

그리고 그는 잽싸게 삽을 집어 들고 감독 앞으로 바

pain-in-the-ass Seung-sik without lifting a finger. Like this."

The man raised the blade of the shovel. They were still easily four feet away from the railing.

Suddenly the supervisor cried, "That son of a bitch was a dirty red. He deserved to die!"

The man would have had time to think and change his mind if it hadn't been for that last word: red. He was unable to control himself, and he swung. The supervisor held onto the railing with all of his might, but at the last moment he let go. He was killed in the same way he'd killed another man, but he took a few hours to die.

The man had only a faint recollection of what he did next. The images were hazy, like in a dream. The dump truck driver shouting, "He's alive! Call an ambulance! Call an ambulance!" and his surrender to the police who came racing to the scene. Only the judge's sentence seemed clear, ringing in his ears. "Fifteen years!"

Around that time, Ik-su returned. The man was sleeping. The boy calmly looked down at him. He caught a glimpse of his father's shaved head where the hat had come halfway off. He carefully righted

싹 다가들었다. 감독은 떡잎처럼 부들부들 떨며 뒤로 물러났다.

"난 삽을 사용하지 않았어."

엉겁결에 감독이 실토한 말이었다.

"바로 그거야. 당신은 나처럼 이렇게 한 발 한 발 다가든 거야. 그러면 등 뒤 감각이 둔하니까 자연히 밀려가다가 실족하게 되는 거지."

그는 삽을 쳐들고 더 바싹 밀어붙였다.

"아니야, 난······."

"물론 당신은 손가락 하나 까딱 않고 그 귀찮은 존재를 없애버릴 수가 있었어. 바로 이렇게."

그는 삽날을 획 내밀었다. 그렇다 해도 난간까지는 1.5미터는 족히 남아 있을 때였다. 별안간 감독이 악을 썼다.

"그놈은 빨갱이야! 죽어 마땅할 놈······."

빨갱이란 말만 하지 않았어도 마음을 돌이킬 여유는 있었다. 그는 참을 수가 없어 삽날을 휘둘렀고, 감독은 떨어지지 않으려고 난간에서 안간힘으로 버티었으나 결국 추락하고 말았다. 감독은 자기가 이용했던 수법과

it and went around to his feet and shook him by the leg. Startled, the man jumped up.

"Dad, what's the matter?"

The boy's eyes were round as if he were startled too. Quickly, the man felt for his hat. It was still on properly. Only then did he smile in embarrassment.

"Here you go, Dad." He handed his father two cigarettes and a matchbook.

"Did you go down to get these?"

The boy nodded, offering him a light.

"I don't need to be smoking them."

The boy held out the match as the man inhaled. Although he let out a long puff of smoke, it still seemed like something hot was caught in his chest. *Eight years to go. On the off chance that I'm pardoned, I'll be out sooner. Until then, Ik-su, grow up healthy and strong. When your dad's a free man, you won't have any worries. Over the past seven years, I've become pretty handy; I've mastered carpentry, welding, and I even know how to use a lathe. When I get out and I really do take a job overseas, I'll be able to send you to university, or on a study abroad program. It's true. I'm confident.* The man took impatient drags on his cigarette.

"Dad, are cigarettes really that good?" Ik-su asked, his face lifted up close to his father's.

똑같은 방법으로 그렇게 죽었다. 비록 몇 시간 후에 숨을 거두긴 했지만.

그는 그 뒤 자신이 어떻게 했는지는 기억이 희미했다. 덤프트럭 기사가 "죽지 않았다! 앰뷸런스! 앰뷸런스!" 하고 소리친 것과 달려온 경찰에 자수한 것은 마치 꿈속같이 아련했지만, 판사의 언도만은 아직도 생생한 이명으로 남아 있었다. 십오 년!

그때쯤 소년이 돌아왔다. 그는 잠들어 있었다. 소년은 가만히 아빠를 내려다보았다. 반쯤 벗겨진 모자 사이로 빡빡 깎인 민머리가 보였다. 소년은 조심스럽게 그 모자를 바로 씌워주고 발치께로 가서 그의 다리를 흔들었다. 그는 소스라쳐 놀라며 벌떡 일어났다.

"아빠, 왜 그래?"

아이도 깜짝 놀랐는지 눈이 둥그레졌다. 그는 재빨리 모자를 만져보았다. 그것은 그대로 잘 씌워져 있었다. 그는 민망한 듯 비로소 웃었다.

"아빠, 이것 피워."

소년이 그에게 담배 두 개비와 성냥을 내밀었다.

"이것 사러 내려갔었니?"

The man nodded.

"When you're ready, let's go to the Botanical Gardens."

"I'm done. Let's go there now." He pocketed the other cigarette and the matches, and disposed of the stub.

The sun started to go down. At around five, they took a bus bound for Gwanghwamun. It was full.

"Dad!" Jostled ahead by the crowd, the boy called to him from inside.

"I'm coming!" He shoved people aside to get further in. But standing in the middle of three or four people was a very overweight middle-aged man blocking the way, and he couldn't pass.

"Dad," his son called again.

"I'm here."

"Come this way."

Once more, he tried pushing by the middle-aged man to get to his son. Pinned tightly in the crowd, the man didn't budge.

"I'm sorry, my son is back there..."

"I don't care if it's your grandfather. You're going to have to wait."

Ik-su called for him a few times in a worried tone, and the man felt around for the boy's hand as

아들이 고개를 끄덕이고 성냥을 내밀었다.

"이런 건 안 피워도 되는데……."

그는 아들이 내미는 성냥불로 담배를 댕겨 물었다. 연기를 길게 내뿜었으나 가슴에 뜨거운 것은 그대로 꽉 막고 있는 것 같았다. 앞으로 팔 년이다. 행여 특사라도 받게 되면 더 빠를 수도 있어. 익수야, 그때까지만 건강하게 자라다오. 아빠가 사회인이 되면 넌 걱정 없다. 지난 칠 년 동안 아빤 목공·용접·선반 기술까지 두루 익혀두었다. 밖에 나와서 정말로 해외 취업이라도 하게 되면 어디 대학뿐이냐, 유학이라도 시켜주마. 정말이란다. 아빤 자신이 있어. 그는 급하게 담배를 빨아댔다.

"아빠, 담배가 그렇게 맛있어?"

아들이 얼굴을 바짝 디밀고 물었다. 그는 고개를 끄덕였다.

"그것 다 피우고 식물원 가자."

"다 피웠다. 얼른 가자꾸나."

그는 남은 담배 한 개비와 성냥을 주머니에 챙겨 넣고 꽁초를 버렸다.

해가 기울기 시작했다. 오후 다섯 시경 그들은 광화문

the bus stopped at Jonggak.

After they transferred to the bus for Suyuri, the boy started to doze off. The day's outing seemed to have exhausted him. The man hugged the sleepy boy close and looked out the window. The sun was sinking behind the buildings to the west. He had until seven. He rubbed his face so hard that it felt like parts of it might crumble off in his hands.

They got off the bus and turned onto a quiet street. Rays from the sun often crossed their path, but the man walked in silence, holding his son's hand. At about the spot where the orphanage came into view, the boy stopped.

"Dad, when are you coming back?"

"Next year... I'll bring a lot of presents with me then," he said, shifting the empty bag on to his shoulder.

"It's okay if you don't. Just come, all right?"

"I'll come. I promise."

The boy paused for a moment and let go of his hand.

"Dad, you go. I have to get back fast and go to sleep because I've got school tomorrow."

"Okay..." The man felt around in his pockets. He had 3,500 *won* left. Keeping 500 *won* for himself, he

행 버스를 탔다. 버스는 만원이었다.

"아빠!"

먼저 밀려들어간 아들이 저 안쪽에서 그를 불렀다.

"오냐, 간다."

그는 사람들을 비집고 안으로 들어갔다. 그러나 두서
너 사람을 사이에 두고 몹시 뚱뚱한 중년 남자가 그들
을 가로막고 있어 더 이상 파고들 수가 없었다.

"아빠."

아들이 다시 그를 불렀다.

"여기 있다."

"어서 와."

그는 아들 곁으로 가려고 다시 한 번 중년 남자를 밀
쳐보았다. 빽빽한 사람들 틈에 낀 그 중년은 꼼짝도 하
지 않았다.

"죄송합니다만, 저쪽에 내 아들이 있어서……."

"아들이 아니라 할아비라도 상황이 이렇잖소, 좀 참으
시오."

소년이 몇 번이나 불안한 목소리로 그를 불렀고 그
역시 아들 쪽으로 연신 손을 더듬는 사이 버스가 종각

handed the boy the rest.

"No. You take it for the bus." The boy drew his hand away, but the man pulled it back, smiling.

"Dad's got more in his inside pocket. When summer comes, you'll want milk and ice cream. You take this money..."

The boy took it, and was the first to turn away. The man held out his hand towards the boy's retreating figure, as if he had something he wanted to say. But the evening sun interfered with his train of thought.

The boy stopped and looked behind him. His father was running hard. He looked like he was bobbing in the air, driven on by the setting sun. The boy bit his lip. *Dad, last winter, I was so worried about you. I heard it was really cold in there...and you sleep on the bare floor without even a blanket. But I know there's no way you'll die on me.*

The boy began to walk, grudgingly. *And Dad, I heard Mom had another baby. But never mind. You've got me.* He raised his head and looked up the hill. Through blurred eyes, he could see the shadow of someone running out from Angel Orphanage.

1) During the Japanese colonial period, the Changgyeong Palace compound in Seoul was developed as a zoo and

앞에 세워졌다.

수유리 쪽 버스를 갈아탄 뒤부터 소년은 졸기 시작했다. 오늘 나들이가 아이에게 피로를 준 모양이었다. 그는 조는 아들을 꼭 끌어안고 차창 밖을 내다보았다. 해가 서쪽 건물 위에서 자맥질하고 있었다. 일곱 시까지야……. 그는 바스러질 듯이 얼굴을 비벼댔다.

버스에서 내려 그들은 한적한 길로 접어들었다. 해가 자꾸 그의 발길을 가로막았지만, 그는 아들의 손을 꼭 잡고 묵묵히 걸었다. 저만큼 고아원 건물이 보일 때쯤 소년이 걸음을 멈추었다.

"아빠, 언제 또 와?"

"내년에……. 그땐 선물 많이 사 올게."

그는 빈 가방을 추스르며 말했다.

"선물 안 사줘도 좋아. 꼭 나오기만 해. 알았지?"

"꼭 나오고말고."

소년은 잠깐 머뭇거리다가 그의 손을 놓아주었다.

"아빠, 어서 가봐. 나도 빨리 가서 자야 내일 학교 가지."

"그래……."

botanical gardens known as Changgyeong Park. In 1983, these recreational facilities were closed, the zoo was moved to Seoul Grand Park in the suburb of Gwacheon, and the palace underwent restoration.

2) Traditionally, it was the custom for adult family members to feel the *gochu* (penis) of a baby or little boy. It was a non-sexual gesture demonstrating one's pride in having male offspring in a culture where boys were preferred.

3) Nanji Island in west Seoul served as the city's landfill site from 1978~1993. The land was reclaimed and developed into the World Cup Park in the lead-up to the 2002 FIFA World Cup, jointly hosted by Korea and Japan.

4) The man pretends to be a stock character in Korean mask dances (*talchum*) named Chwibari, who represents the common people. Chwibari has a red face, a wrinkled forehead, and a shock of hair, and is known for strutting when he walks.

5) Beginning in the 1970s, civil defense drills were held in the afternoon for half an hour on the 15th day of every month in preparation for a North Korean attack. Sirens sounded and workers stopped what they were doing, took shelter in a designated spot, and waited for directions from the civil defense corps, which were given via loudspeaker or over the radio. Since 1989, the number of drills per year has been gradually reduced.

6) Hiring in the construction and shipbuilding industries was sometimes handled through foreman subcontracting. As practiced within this system, the foreman was not a permanent worker, but competed with other foremen for a temporary position at a company. He was responsible not only for overseeing the work of laborers at a work site, but also for hiring and paying them. In 2008, President Roh Moo-hyeon outlawed this system of recruitment and labor management.

Translated by Kari Schenk

그는 주머니를 뒤졌다. 삼천오백 원이 남아 있었다. 그는 오백 원을 남기고 삼천 원을 아들 손에 쥐어주었다.

"싫어. 아빠 차 타고 가야지."

소년이 손을 감추었다. 그는 웃으며 아이의 손을 끌어냈다.

"아빤 안주머니에 또 있어. 여름이 오면 우유도 먹고 싶고 아이스크림도 먹고 싶을 텐데, 우선 이 돈 갖고……."

소년이 돈을 받아 쥐고 먼저 돌아섰다. 그는 무슨 말인가 꼭 할 이야기가 있을 것 같아 아들의 등을 향해 손을 내밀었다. 그러나 저녁 햇살이 그 생각을 가로막았다.

소년은 걸음을 멈추었다. 그리고 뒤를 돌아다보았다. 급하게 뛰어가는 아빠의 모습은 마치 석양에 둥둥 밀려가는 듯했다. 소년은 입술을 깨물었다. 아빠, 지난겨울에 난 아빠 걱정을 얼마나 했는지 몰라. 그 안엔 몹시 춥다던데……. 이불도 없이 맨마루에 잔다며? 그래도 난 알고 있어. 우리 아빤 절대로 죽지 않는다는 걸.

소년은 토달토달 걷기 시작했다. 그리고 참 아빠, 엄만 또 아기를 낳았대. 잊어버려. 내가 있잖아. 소년은 고개를 들어 언덕 위를 바라보았다. '천사고아원'에서 누군가가 달려나오는 모습이 뿌옇게 흔들려 보였다.

『밤길』, 책세상, 2009

해설

Afterword

아버지와 아들의 애틋한 공감

고인환 (문학평론가)

    윤정모의 「아들」은 아버지와 아들의 애틋한 공감과 소통을 형상화한 단편이다. 드라마틱한 상황을 차분한 어조의 문체로 갈무리한 수작(秀作)이다. 아버지는 살인죄로 15년을 선고받고 7년째 수감 중이다. 네 살 때 헤어진 아들은 어미에게 버림받고 고아원에서 자라고 있다. 「아들」은 이 둘이 만나는 짧은 하루의 이야기이다. '7년 모범수'에게 하루의 '특박'이 허용된다는 사실을 안 아버지가 출소자 인편으로 아들이 있는 고아원에 편지를 보낸다. 열 한 살의 아들에게 아버지는 외국(사우디아라비아)에 돈 벌러 나간 것으로 알려져 있다.

    윤정모는 이러한 표충적 서사구조에 우리의 열악한

Father and Son: A Story of Sympathy

Ko In-hwan (literary critic)

Yoon jung-mo's "Father and Son" is a poignant story that deals with the sympathy and special kind of communication that exists between father and son. It is an excellent work of fiction that presents a highly dramatic situation in a serene, almost matter-of-fact style. Where Yoon's story may differ from similar father/son stories, however, is in the unique backgrounds of its titular characters. At the story's beginning, the father in Yoon's work has been in prison for seven years of a fifteen-year murder sentence. His son, separated from the father at only four, now lives in an orphanage after being abandoned by his mother. The story, then,

노동 현실을 섬세하게 직조하고 있다. 한 가정이 붕괴되는 기구한 사연과 산업화 시대의 모순을 포개 놓고 있는 셈이다. 작가는 아버지와 아들의 내면적 소통을 통해 절망적 현실 속에서 피어나는 가느다란 희망의 메시지를 길어 올리고 있다.

아버지의 사연을 따라가보자. 그는 소박한 꿈을 지닌 평범한 가장이었다. 막노동판에서 잔뼈가 굵은 아버지는 건설회사 소속으로 근무할 때 아내를 만나 아이를 낳고 작은 전세방을 얻어 오순도순 살았다. 좋은 아빠가 되는 것이 꿈이었다.

그러던 어느 날 고향 친구 승식이 찾아온다. 승식은 노조를 결성하여 활동하다가 강제퇴직을 당했다. 노조를 허용하지 않겠다는 회사의 탄압과 회유에 맞서다가 실직한 것이다. 승식은 회사를 노동청에 고발하고 일자리를 찾아 친구를 찾아온 것이다. 그러던 승식이 기술자로서가 아니라 공사장 노무자로 죽고 말았다. 공사판 또한 부정과 부패가 만연했다. 현장 감독은 자신의 지위를 이용해 노동자들을 착취하고 있었다. 그는 다음 공사의 일자리를 미끼로 노무자들에게 뇌물을 받아 챙긴다. 그런데 그 약속을 지킬 수 없게 되었다고 엄포를

deals with their meeting for a single day, a privilege the father learns is granted for every "seven-year model prisoner," one "special day out." The father sends a letter through a released prisoner to arrange this meeting with his son. The son, now eleven years old, believes his father works abroad (Saudi Arabia) to make money, as that is what his mother told him.

Moreover, Yoon skillfully weaves another story within "Father and Son's" main narrative. It is a story grounded in the poor working conditions of Korea, a story of one family's unfortunate collapse and its struggles within the societal contradictions of the modern industrialization period of Korea. And yet through the intimate communications between this father and son, Yoon nurtures a message of budding hope out of "Father and Son's" desperate reality.

Consider the father's story. Once an ordinary household head with simple dreams, the father meets his wife after years working as a day laborer at a local construction company. They live happily with a baby at a rented housing, his only dream to be a good father.

One day, however, his hometown friend, Seung-

놓는다. 승식은 이러한 감독에게 항의하다가 삼 층에서 떨어져 죽었다. 전후 사정을 알아본 화자는 현장 감독을 찾아간다. 감독은 승식을 '불순분자'이자 '빨갱이'며 '죽어 마땅할 놈'이라 말한다. '빨갱이'란 말에 격분한 화자는 '삽날'을 휘둘렀다. 감독은 떨어지지 않으려고 난간에서 버티다가 결국 추락하고 만다. 감독은 자신이 승식에게 했던 방법과 똑같은 방식으로 죽었다.

7년 전의 일이다. 지난 칠 년 동안 감옥에서 '목공―용접―선반' 등 사회생활에 필요한 제반 기술을 두루 익혔다. 8년 후면 사회로 나올 것이다. 아들이 그때까지 건강하게 자라주기를 바랄 뿐이다.

이제 아들과 헤어질 시간이다. 저만치 '고아원' 건물이 보인다. '돈을 받아 쥐고 먼저' 돌아서는 아들에게 '무슨 말인가 꼭 할 이야기가 있을 것 같아' 손을 내밀었으나 '저녁 햇살이 그 생각'을 가로막는다. 이윽고 아들이 돌아본다.

소년은 걸음을 멈추었다. 그리고 뒤를 돌아다보았다. 급하게 뛰어가는 아빠의 모습은 마치 석양에 둥둥 밀려가는 듯했다. 아빠, 지난겨울에 난 아빠 걱정을 얼마나

sik comes to visit him. Seung-sik has been fired after participating in the organization of a labor union and after fighting against his company's oppression as well as their attempts to win him over. Seung-sik visits his friend after lodging a complaint against his company at the Ministry of Labor. That same Seung-sik, though, dies as a day laborer, not as a technician, at a construction site where corrupt and unjust practices run rampant. These corrupt practices, the reader discovers, involve extorting laborers by promising future work, upon which the field overseer then simply reneges on his promises whenever convenient. It is Seung-sik who protests this and subsequently falls to his death from the third floor of a partially constructed building under suspicious circumstance. After learning these details, the father visits the field overseer who defends himself by further vilifying his friend calling him an "impure element," a "red," and a "son-of-a-bitch deserving to die." Enraged, the father attacks him with a shovel and the overseer ends up falling to his death, ironically dying the same way as Seung-sik despite their radically opposed views and circumstances.

As the father spends a painfully short day with his

했는지 몰라. 그 안엔 몹시 춥다던데……. 이불도 없이 맨마루에 잔다며? 그래도 난 알고 있어. 우리 아빠 절대로 죽지 않는다는 걸.

소년은 토달토달 걷기 시작했다. 그리고 참 아빠, 엄마 또 아기를 낳았대. 잊어버려. 내가 있잖아. 소년은 고개를 들어 언덕 위를 바라보았다. '천사고아원'에서 누군가가 달려나오는 모습이 뿌옇게 흔들려 보였다(76~78쪽).

아버지의 사랑에 응답하는 아들의 사려 깊은 마음씀씀이가 눈시울을 적시게 하는 장면이다. 이렇듯 윤정모의 「아들」은 아버지와 아들의 눈물겨운 공감과 소통의 무늬를 애틋한 어조로 포착한 작품이다.

son, the father recollects these events from seven years ago. Prior to this meeting, we learn the father has learned various useful skills in prison such as woodworking, welding, and lathing, and that he will be released in eight more years. His and his son's situation is heartbreaking, but the father maintains his only wish is for his son to grow up healthy.

"Father and Son" ends on a particularly poignant moment, one that surprises its readers and even further deepens its pathos. As the time for them to part each draws near, the father thrusts his hand into his son's, attempting to hand him the last petty cash he possesses, and feeling the desperate urge to say a few last heartfelt words to his son. The evening sun blocks the father's thoughts, though, and finally the son turns around.

The boy stopped and looked behind him. His father was running hard. He looked like he was bobbing in the air, driven on by the setting sun. The boy bit his lip. *Dad, last winter, I was so worried about you. I heard it was really cold in there...and you sleep on the bare floor without even a blanket. But I know there's no way you'll die on me.*

The boy began to walk, grudgingly. *And Dad, I*

heard Mom had another baby. But never mind. You've got me. He raised his head and looked up the hill. Through blurred eyes, he could see the shadow of someone running out from the Angel Orphanage.

In a surprising reversal, the son's thoughtful consideration of his father's love proves to be perhaps, the most heart-wrenching. Yoon jung-mo's "Father and Son" is a small, but moving masterpiece, perfectly capturing the poignant patterns of sympathy and understanding that lay between a father and his son.

비평의 목소리

Critical Acclaim

후배들이 윤정모를 좋아하고 신뢰하는 진정한 이유는 온갖 악조건 속에서 온몸을 던져 치열하게 개척해 온 그의 문학적 지평 때문이다. 독자로서『님』과『고삐』와『사랑』의 책갈피에 눈물을 번지며 읽었던 우리들은 그의 그 작은 몸짓 어디에 그 큰 슬픔과 처연한 투혼이 감추어져 있는지 놀라울 따름이었다. 그의 문학적 연대기는 문학예술이 결코 경제적으로 배부르고 정신적으로 안락한 자들의 앞마당이 아니며 소설이란 세상의 그늘진 곳에서 상처받고 있는 인간의 영혼으로부터 그 힘을 얻어간다는 진실을 입증하는 살아 있는 증거들이었다.

방현석, 「시리도록 선명한 문학적 긍지」,

We, junior writers truly love and trust Yoon jung-mo because she has been exploring new literary horizons by throwing her entire self into the task and defying all sorts of personal hardships. When reading her *Lover*, *Reins*, and *Love,* tears fill our eyes and we are simply amazed by the great sadness and somber fighter spirit hidden beneath even her smallest gestures. The history of her literary achievements is living proof of the truth that literary arts can never be the playground for the wealthy and mentally comfortable; they feed on wounded human spirits suffering in the dark underbelly of the world.

《실천문학》, 1996년 겨울호.

윤정모의 작품에는 때기름 짙게 배인 작업복이나 더득더득 붙은 무명옷 소맷자락으로 눈물을 닦는 쓰라림이 스며 있다. 기나긴 인종과 체념의 세월을 겪은 뒤에 터뜨리는 통곡은 끝내 분노로 바뀌어 포효하는, 근육질이 조화롭게 발달한 갑오농민전쟁의 군중벽화를 연상시킨다. 그들은 원한과 울화 속에서 녹두꽃이 떨어지고 청포장수가 울고 가도 구릿빛 얼굴에 흰 이를 드러내 놓고 크게 웃으며 혁명적 낙관주의를 전망케 만든다. 80년대 후반기 이후에 우리에게 윤정모는 민족민중문학의 얼마나 든든한 보루이자 초병이며 수색대의 앞장이었던가!

임헌영, 「우리 시대의 거울로서의 윤정모」,

『우리 시대의 소설 읽기』, 도서출판 글, 1992.

매춘 생활을 통해 연명해 나갈 수밖에 없는 자매의 비통한 인생사를 서사의 중심 골격으로 삼아 전개되는 『고삐』는, 미국에 종속된 한국의 비틀린 역사적 현실을 과학적으로 인식해낸다. 하여 미국에 종속되어 가는 한

Bang Hyeon-seok, "Pride of Literature, So Lucid, Almost Chilly," *Silcheonmunhak*, Winter, 1996.

Yoon jung-mo's works are pervaded with the bitterness of those who must wipe their tears with the sleeves of their greasy work gears and tattered cotton clothes. The sound of wailing after lengthy years of patient obedience and resignation reminds me of a Gabo Peasant Revolution mural, always featuring roaring mobs of heavily muscled people. But these are the people who enable us to main-tain revolutionary optimism, those copper-faced people who can laugh out loud, displaying all their white teeth, even when the "mung bean flowers fall and mung bean jelly peddlers weep."[1] Since the 1980s and on, what a bastion and forward scout for the national people's literature movement Yoon has been!

Lim Heon-yeong, "Yoon Jung-mo as a Mirror of Our Times," *Reading Fiction of Our Times* (Seoul: Geul, 1992)

Reins, a story centered around the bitter lives of two sisters who must depend on prostitution for their survival, offers an empirical understanding of Korean historical reality distorted through its sub-

국의 부끄러운 자화상을 있는 그대로 드러낼 뿐만 아니라, 미국의 폭압적 힘으로부터 벗어나고자 하는 반외세 문학의 기치를 내건다. 윤정모의 이러한 작업은 한반도에서 온갖 핍박과 역사적 질곡 속에 살아갈 수밖에 없는 한국 여성의 뿌리 뽑힌 삶의 현실에 대한 절절한 육성의 증언인 바, 이처럼 씻을 수 없는 오욕의 상처를 안겨준 한반도의 제국주의적 광폭성을 증언하고, 더 나아가 한반도에서 일체의 제국주의적 흔적을 남겨놓지 않으려는 작가의 저항적 의지 그 자체라 해도 과언이 아닐 터이다.

고명철, 「미국의 전횡적 힘의 논리를 전복시키는 우리 소설」,

『칼날 위에 서다』, 실천문학, 2005.

참된 이념의 부재는 무수한 사실들을 허공 속에 부유하게 만든다. 이것이 사실에 충실한 소설들이 갈수록 재미없어지고 여러 작가들이 재미를 찾아 사실주의를 포기하도록 유혹받는 현상을 설명해 줄 것이다. 그러나 윤정모의 『들』은 사실주의를 고수하면서도 이러한 대세를 거슬러 나아간다. 이 소설은 겉멋 든 관념이나 엽기적 이야기, 사실 폭로를 주무기로 하는 소설들과는 다

jection to the US. It not only presents Korea's shameful self-portrait as it really is but also bears the standard of literature against foreign influences. This work of Yoon jung-mo's is an eyewitness account of the uprooted lives of the Korean women who have had no choice but to lead strained, historically fettered lives. As a testimony to the imperialist violence in the Korean peninsula, one that has left us with incurable and dishonorable wounds, it wouldn't be an exaggeration to say that this novel is itself the author's will to resist and wipe away all imperialist traces from the Korean peninsula.

Go Myeong-cheol, "Our Fiction: Subversive of the Despotic Logic of the U.S.," *Standing on a Knife Blade*

(Seoul: Silcheonmunhak, 2005)

Absence of true ideology leaves nothing but innumerable facts to float and hang in the air. This explains why novels faithful to reality have become more and more uninteresting to readers and why many writers have been tempted to forfeit realism in search of more exciting, surreal avenues. Yoon jung-mo's *The Fields*, however, resists this contemporary trend and continues to adhere to realism. It pursues a kind of excitement different from novels

른 종류의 재미를 추구한다. 그것은 현실적 인물의 호흡을 통해 우리의 삶에 '역사'라는 차원이 존재함을 느낄 때에만 맛볼 수 있는 재미이다.

김성호, 「들」, 창작과비평사, 1992.

「아들」은 아버지와 아들이라는 동성 사이의 깊은 이해와 공감의 시간들을 그리고 있는 작품이다. 앞에서 살펴본 어머니와 딸 사이에 보인 원망과 자책의 거리와는 완전히 다르다. 그리고 서술자의 간섭이 거의 없는 상태에서 주체인 남성들의 공감과 이해의 시간이 펼쳐진다. 서술자는 원거리에서 아들과 아버지의 모습을 그리고, 이후 자유롭게 번갈아 이어지는 아버지와 아들의 과거 회상을 독자와 함께 지켜볼 뿐이다. 회상을 통해 두 주인물의 내면과 지나온 시간들은 조리 있게 펼쳐진다. 그리고 그들의 대화는 서로를 배려하는 가운데 내밀하고 비밀스런 이해와 공감의 장이 된다.

정미숙, 「여성 부정과 여성 소외-윤정모 소설의 서술 분석」,
『현대문학이론연구』, 현대문학이론학회, 2001.

armed with supercilious ideas, bizarre narratives, or muckraking events. It produces the kind of excitement we experience only when we feel the "historical" dimension of fiction, stories that deal with nothing less than breathing, living, real human beings.

Kim Seong-ho, *Deul* [Fields] (Paju: Changbi, 1992)

"Father and Son" depicts the profound male-male understanding and sympathy between father and son⋯ While the narrator rarely intervenes, a period of sympathy and understanding between the two male subjects unfolds. The narrator describes their actions and thoughts from a distance and simply observes their freely interweaving recollections together with readers. Through these flashbacks the two main characters' interior worlds and pasts evolve coherently. And their conversation and consideration for each other becomes the space for their deepest and secret understanding and sympathy.

Jeong Mi-suk, "Negation and Alienation of Women: An Analysis of Yoon Jung-mo's Fiction," *The Journal of Modern Literary Theory* (The Society of Modern Literary Theory, 2001)

1) The phrase "mung bean flowers fall and mung bean jelly peddlers cry" refers to a folksong about the failure of the Gabo Peasant Revolution.

윤정모

    윤정모는 1946년 경북 월성에서 태어났다. 부산 혜화여고를 거쳐 서라벌예술대학교 문예창작학과를 졸업했다. 1968년 장편 『무늬져 부는 바람』을 출간하면서 작품 활동을 시작하였다. 1981년 《여성중앙》 중편 현상공모에 「바람벽의 딸들」이 당선되어 정식으로 문단에 데뷔하였다.

    1980년 광주민중항쟁을 직간접적으로 겪으며 우리 민족사의 현장, 비극적 분단 현실, 계층 간의 갈등 문제, 여성의 수난사 등을 본격적으로 탐색하기 시작하였다. 「등나무」(1983), 「밤길」(1985), 「님」(1985), 『고삐』(1988) 등 1980년대를 대표하는 작품들은 광주민중항쟁에서 비롯된 분노와 저항감을 문학적으로 껴안으려는 열정의 소산이었다.

    윤정모는 1990년대 이후 보다 넓은 시각으로 역사와 시대 현실의 문제를 다루기 시작한다. 그의 소설은 어둡고 암울한 현실에서 희망을 길어 올리려는 치열한 비판 정신에서 비롯된다. 이는 강렬한 역사의식으로 표상

Yoon jung-mo

Yoon jung-mo was born in Wolseong, Korea in 1946. After graduating from Hyehwa Girls High School in Busan and the Department of Creative Writing at Seorabol Art College, she began her literary career when her novel *Pattered Winds* was published in 1968. She later made her official literary debut in 1981 when her novella *Daughters of Walls* won the *Women Joongang* Novella Contest.

Since her direct and indirect experiences with the 1980 Gwangju Rebellion, she began to fully explore scenes from her national history that dealt with the country's tragic division, class conflict, and women's history. Her 1980s works, including "Wisteria (1983)," "Night Road (1985)," "Lover (1985)," and *Reins* (1988), originated during this period from which she began her passionate literary embrace of the anger and antipathy of the Gwangju Rebellion.

After the 1990s, Yoon began to deal with history and reality from a broader perspective than before. Her novels now come from a fierce critical spirit that tries to find hope within even the darkest,

되고 있는데 부정한 시대현실을 극복하려는 작가의식의 산물이다. 또한 윤정모의 소설은 '나'에게서 출발하여 '너' 그리고 '우리'로 확장되는 원심력을 지닌다. 그의 소설은 일상 속으로 깊이 스며들어 민중들의 섬세한 삶의 무늬를 따뜻하게 감싸 안는다. 이는 당대 민중들의 삶에 대한 관심에 다름 아니며 여기에는 훈훈한 휴머니즘의 정신이 깃들어 있다. 이렇듯, 그의 소설이 주는 감동은 민초들의 삶을 따스한 사랑으로 감싸는 작가의 넓은 가슴과 끊임없는 부정의 정신으로 현실을 초극하려는 치열한 역사의식에서 비롯된다. 그의 소설은 고통과 절망을 디디고 선 작품이기에 아름답다.

농촌 현실의 사회, 구조적 모순을 총체적으로 형상화한『들』(1992), 윤이상의 삶에 투영된 예술적 성취와 민족사적 엇갈림을 서사화한『나비의 꿈』(1996), 한국과 아일랜드의 비극적 현실에 투영된 젊은이들의 고뇌와 방황을 다룬『슬픈 아일랜드』(2000), 한 노인의 힘겨운 삶을 통해 질곡의 한국 현대사를 증언하고 있는『꾸야 삼촌』(2002), 수메르 문명에 대한 끈질긴 탐색의 결과물인『수메리안』(2005), 『길가메시』(2007), 『수메르』(2010) 등은 그의 작가의식을 잘 보여주는 작품들이다. 최근에는 일

most depressing realities. This spirit is embodied in her intense historical consciousness, a product of her authorial consciousness to overcome injustice in reality. In addition, Yoon's novels centrifugally expand from the "I" to the "you," and finally to the "we." Her novels guide us deep into the everyday lives of ordinary people and leave us warmly embracing their fine details. They reflect the author's warm, humanist spirit and her profound interest in the lives of ordinary people. Her works allow us to travel through Yoon's generous heart, which wraps grassroots sentiments with warmth and tenderness as well as a fierce historical consciousness that pushes Yoon forward to overcome reality through the spirit of everlasting negation. Yoon's novels are beautiful because they are born of pain and despair.

Her representative works include *The Fields* (1992), a novel encompassing the contradictory aspects of contemporary agricultural reality; *Butterfly's Dreams* (1996), a novel that depicts the conflicts between Yoon Isang's artistic life and national history; *Sorrowful Ireland* (2000), a novel on the anguish of the lost and the young within the tragic realities of Korea and Ireland; *Uncle Gguya* (2002), a novel that

본군 위안부 문제를 정면으로 다룬「에미 이름은 조센 삐였다」(1982)를「봉선화」로 각색하여 연극무대에 올리기도 했다. 윤정모의 작품은 체험이나 취재를 통해 획득한 역사적 진실성을 생동감 넘치는 문체로 형상화함으로써 빼어난 문학적 성취를 이루었다는 평가를 받고 있다.

1988년 신동엽 창작기금을 받았다. 단재문학상(1993), 서라벌문학상(1996) 등을 수상하였다. 2002년에 민족문학작가회의(현 한국작가회의) 부이사장을 역임하였다.

testifies to Korea's fettered modern history through the story of one elderly man's difficult life; and *Sumerian* (2005), *Gilgamesh* (2007), and *Sumer* (2010), the results of Yoon's tireless interest in Sumerian civilization. Recently, she also adapted her short story "Mother's Name was Josenbbi (1982)" into a play entitled *Touch-me-not*, which has just recently been put on major stages.

Yoon's works have been critically recognized for their superb literary achievement in depicting historical reality in a number of vivid styles. She received the 1988 Shin Dong-yeop Creative Fund, the Danjae Literary Award (1993), and the Seorabol Literary Award (1996). Finally, she worked as the vice-president of the Writers Association for National Literature (currently, Korean Writers Association) in 2002.

번역 **쉥크 카리** Translated by Kari Schenk

쉥크 카리는 2006년 코리아 타임즈에서 주최하는 한국 문학 번역 수상식에서 추천상을 공동 수상했다. 그녀는 번역 아틀리에와 번역자 특별 수업에 참여하면서 LTI 코리아 스폰서십으로부터 지원을 받았다. 조경란 『국자 이야기』의 번역에 지원금을 받기도 했다. 여러 해 동안 그녀는 고려대학교에서 영어 학업 기술에 관한 강의를 하고 있다.

Kari Schenk was the co-winner of the Commendation Prize in the 2006 *Korea Times* Modern Korean Literature Translation Awards. She has benefited from the sponsorship of LTI Korea, taking the special class for translators, participating in the Translation Atelier, and receiving a grant to translate Jo Kyung-ran's *The Story of a Ladle* in 2011. For many years, she has been working at Korea University, where she is currently teaching English academic skills classes.

감수 **전승희, 데이비드 윌리엄 홍**
Edited by Jeon Seung-hee and David William Hong

전승희는 서울대학교와 하버드대학교에서 영문학과 비교문학으로 박사 학위를 받았으며, 현재 하버드대학교 한국학 연구소의 연구원으로 재직하며 아시아 문예 계간지 《ASIA》 편집위원으로 활동 중이다. 현대 한국문학 및 세계문학을 다룬 논문을 다수 발표했으며, 바흐친의 『장편소설과 민중언어』, 제인 오스틴의 『오만과 편견』 등을 공역했다. 1988년 한국여성연구소의 창립과 《여성과 사회》의 창간에 참여했고, 2002년부터 보스턴 지역 피학대 여성을 위한 단체인 '트랜지션하우스' 운영에 참여해 왔다. 2006년 하버드대학교 한국학 연구소에서 '한국 현대사와 기억'을 주제로 한 워크숍을 주관했다.

Jeon Seung-hee is a member of the Editorial Board of *ASIA*, is a Fellow at the Korea Institute, Harvard University. She received a Ph.D. in English Literature from Seoul National University and a Ph.D. in Comparative Literature from Harvard University. She has presented and published numerous papers on modern Korean and world literature. She is also a co-translator of Mikhail Bakhtin's *Novel and the People's Culture* and Jane Austen's *Pride and Prejudice*. She is a founding member of the Korean Women's Studies Institute and of the biannual Women's Studies' journal *Women and Society* (1988), and she has been working at 'Transition House,' the first and oldest shelter for battered women in New England. She organized a workshop entitled "The Politics of Memory in Modern Korea" at the Korea Institute,

Harvard University, in 2006. She also served as an advising committee member for the Asia-Africa Literature Festival in 2007 and for the POSCO Asian Literature Forum in 2008.

데이비드 윌리엄 홍은 미국 일리노이주 시카고에서 태어났다. 일리노이대학교에서 영문학을, 뉴욕대학교에서 영어교육을 공부했다. 지난 2년간 서울에 거주하면서 처음으로 한국인과 아시아계 미국인 문학에 깊이 몰두할 기회를 가졌다. 현재 뉴욕에서 거주하며 강의와 저술 활동을 한다.

David William Hong was born in 1986 in Chicago, Illinois. He studied English Literature at the University of Illinois and English Education at New York University. For the past two years, he lived in Seoul, South Korea, where he was able to immerse himself in Korean and Asian-American literature for the first time. Currently, he lives in New York City, teaching and writing.

바이링궐 에디션 한국 대표 소설 077

아들

2014년 11월 14일 초판 1쇄 발행

지은이 윤정모 | 옮긴이 쉥크 카리 | 펴낸이 김재범
감수 전승희, 데이비드 윌리엄 홍 | 기획위원 정은경, 전성태, 이경재
편집 정수인, 이은혜, 김형욱, 윤단비 | 관리 박신영 | 디자인 이춘희
펴낸곳 (주)아시아 | 출판등록 2006년 1월 27일 제406-2006-000004호
주소 서울특별시 동작구 서달로 161-1(흑석동 100-16)
전화 02.821.5055 | 팩스 02.821.5057 | 홈페이지 www.bookasia.org
ISBN 979-11-5662-049-5 (set) | 979-11-5662-051-8 (04810)
값은 뒤표지에 있습니다.

Bi-lingual Edition Modern Korean Literature 077

Father and Son

Written by Yoon Jung-mo | **Translated by** Kari Schenk
Published by Asia Publishers | 161-1, Seodal-ro, Dongjak-gu, Seoul, Korea
Homepage Address www.bookasia.org | **Tel.** (822).821.5055 | **Fax.** (822).821.5057
First published in Korea by Asia Publishers 2014
ISBN 979-11-5662-049-5 (set) | 979-11-5662-051-8 (04810)

바이링궐 에디션 한국 대표 소설

한국문학의 가장 중요하고 첨예한 문제의식을 가진 작가들의 대표작을 주제별로 선정!
하버드 한국학 연구원 및 세계 각국의 한국문학 전문 번역진이 참여한 번역 시리즈!
미국 하버드대학교와 컬럼비아대학교 동아시아학과, 캐나다 브리티시컬럼비아대학교 아시아
학과 등 해외 대학에서 교재로 채택!

바이링궐 에디션 한국 대표 소설 set 1

분단 Division

01 병신과 머저리-이청준 The Wounded-Yi Cheong-jun

02 어둠의 혼-김원일 Soul of Darkness-Kim Won-il

03 순이삼촌-현기영 Sun-i Samch'on-Hyun Ki-young

04 엄마의 말뚝 1-박완서 Mother's Stake I-Park Wan-suh

05 유형의 땅-조정래 The Land of the Banished-Jo Jung-rae

산업화 Industrialization

06 무진기행-김승옥 Record of a Journey to Mujin-Kim Seung-ok

07 삼포 가는 길-황석영 The Road to Sampo-Hwang Sok-yong

08 아홉 켤레의 구두로 남은 사내-윤흥길 The Man Who Was Left as Nine Pairs
of Shoes-Yun Heung-gil

09 돌아온 우리의 친구-신상웅 Our Friend's Homecoming-Shin Sang-ung

10 원미동 시인-양귀자 The Poet of Wŏnmi-dong-Yang Kwi-ja

여성 Women

11 중국인 거리-오정희 Chinatown-Oh Jung-hee

12 풍금이 있던 자리-신경숙 The Place Where the Harmonium Was-Shin
Kyung-sook

13 하나코는 없다-최윤 The Last of Hanak'o-Ch'oe Yun

14 인간에 대한 예의-공지영 Human Decency-Gong Ji-young

15 빈처-은희경 Poor Man's Wife-Eun Hee-kyung

바이링궐 에디션 한국 대표 소설 set 2

자유 Liberty

16 필론의 돼지-이문열 Pilon's Pig-Yi Mun-yol

17 슬로우 불릿-이대환 Slow Bullet-Lee Dae-hwan

18 직선과 독가스-임철우 Straight Lines and Poison Gas-Lim Chul-woo

19 깃발-홍희담 The Flag-Hong Hee-dam

20 새벽 출정-방현석 Off to Battle at Dawn-Bang Hyeon-seok

사랑과 연애 Love and Love Affairs

21 별을 사랑하는 마음으로-**윤후명** With the Love for the Stars-**Yun Hu-myong**

22 목련공원-**이승우** Magnolia Park-**Lee Seung-u**

23 칼에 찔린 자국-**김인숙** Stab-**Kim In-suk**

24 회복하는 인간-**한강** Convalescence-**Han Kang**

25 트렁크-**정이현** In the Trunk-**Jeong Yi-hyun**

남과 북 South and North

26 판문점-**이호철** Panmunjom-**Yi Ho-chol**

27 수난 이대-**하근찬** The Suffering of Two Generations-**Ha Geun-chan**

28 분지-**남정현** Land of Excrement-**Nam Jung-hyun**

29 봄 실상사-**정도상** Spring at Silsangsa Temple-**Jeong Do-sang**

30 은행나무 사랑-**김하기** Gingko Love-**Kim Ha-kee**

바이링궐 에디션 한국 대표 소설 set 3

서울 Seoul

31 눈사람 속의 검은 항아리-**김소진** The Dark Jar within the Snowman-**Kim So-jin**

32 오후, 가로지르다-**하성란** Traversing Afternoon-**Ha Seong-nan**

33 나는 봉천동에 산다-**조경란** I Live in Bongcheon-dong-**Jo Kyung-ran**

34 그렇습니까? 기린입니다-**박민규** Is That So? I'm A Giraffe-**Park Min-gyu**

35 성탄특선-**김애란** Christmas Specials-**Kim Ae-ran**

전통 Tradition

36 무자년의 가을 사흘-**서정인** Three Days of Autumn, 1948-**Su Jung-in**

37 유자소전-**이문구** A Brief Biography of Yuja-**Yi Mun-gu**

38 향기로운 우물 이야기-**박범신** The Fragrant Well-**Park Bum-shin**

39 월행-**송기원** A Journey under the Moonlight-**Song Ki-won**

40 협죽도 그늘 아래-**성석제** In the Shade of the Oleander-**Song Sok-ze**

아방가르드 Avant-garde

41 아겔다마-**박상륭** Akeldama-**Park Sang-ryoong**

42 내 영혼의 우물-**최인석** A Well in My Soul-**Choi In-seok**

43 당신에 대해서-**이인성** On You-**Yi In-seong**

44 회색 時-**배수아** Time In Gray-**Bae Su-ah**

45 브라운 부인-**정영문** Mrs. Brown-**Jung Young-moon**

바이링궐 에디션 한국 대표 소설 set 4

디아스포라 Diaspora

46 속옷-김남일 Underwear-Kim Nam-il

47 상하이에 두고 온 사람들-공선옥 People I Left in Shanghai-Gong Sun-ok

48 모두에게 복된 새해-김연수 Happy New Year to Everyone-Kim Yeon-su

49 코끼리-김재영 The Elephant-Kim Jae-young

50 먼지별-이경 Dust Star-Lee Kyung

가족 Family

51 혜자의 눈꽃-천승세 Hye-ja's Snow-Flowers-Chun Seung-sei

52 아베의 가족-전상국 Ahbe's Family-Jeon Sang-guk

53 문 앞에서-이동하 Outside the Door-Lee Dong-ha

54 그리고, 축제-이혜경 And Then the Festival-Lee Hye-kyung

55 봄밤-권여선 Spring Night-Kwon Yeo-sun

유머 Humor

56 오늘의 운세-한창훈 Today's Fortune-Han Chang-hoon

57 새-전성태 Bird-Jeon Sung-tae

58 밀수록 다시 가까워지는-이기호 So Far, and Yet So Near-Lee Ki-ho

59 유리방패-김중혁 The Glass Shield-Kim Jung-hyuk

60 전당포를 찾아서-김종광 The Pawnshop Chase-Kim Chong-kwang

바이링궐 에디션 한국 대표 소설 set 5

관계 Relationship

61 도둑견습 - 김주영 Robbery Training-Kim Joo-young

62 사랑하라, 희망 없이 - 윤영수 Love, Hopelessly-Yun Young-su

63 봄날 오후, 과부 셋 - 정지아 Spring Afternoon, Three Widows-Jeong Ji-a

64 유턴 지점에 보물지도를 묻다 - 윤성희 Burying a Treasure Map at the U-turn-Yoon Sung-hee

65 쁘이거나 쓰이거나 - 백가흠 Puy, Thuy, Whatever-Paik Ga-huim

일상의 발견 Discovering Everyday Life

66 나는 음식이다 - 오수연 I Am Food-Oh Soo-yeon

67 트럭 - 강영숙 Truck-Kang Young-sook

68 통조림 공장 - 편혜영 The Canning Factory-Pyun Hye-young

69 꽃 - 부희령 Flowers-Pu Hee-ryoung

70 피의일요일 - 윤이형 BloodySunday-Yun I-hyeong

금기와 욕망 Taboo and Desire

71 북소리 - **송영** Drumbeat-**Song Yong**

72 발칸의 장미를 내게 주었네 - **정미경** He Gave Me Roses of the Balkans-**Jung Mi-kyung**

73 아무도 돌아오지 않는 밤 - **김숨** The Night Nobody Returns Home-**Kim Soom**

74 젓가락여자 - **천운영** Chopstick Woman-**Cheon Un-yeong**

75 아직 일어나지 않은 일 - **김미월** What Has Yet to Happen-**Kim Mi-wol**